Peppermint Sticks
and
Banana Peels

By
Betty Ingram

Copyright © 2006 by Betty Ingram

ISBN 0-7414-3405-9

Cover drawing by Elizabeth Ingram Guerette

Published by:

INFI∞ITY
PUBLISHING.COM

*1094 New DeHaven Street, Suite 100
West Conshohocken, PA 19428-2713
Info@buybooksontheweb.com
www.buybooksontheweb.com
Toll-free (877) BUY BOOK
Local Phone (610) 941-9999
Fax (610) 941-9959*

Printed in the United States of America

Printed on Recycled Paper

Published August 2006

This book is dedicated to my husband Vic and to my daughters Jean, Vicki, Gayle and Kelli for their patience and guidance

Note:

Some of the writings in this book are from my imagination. Some were written for my family and friends. Others were created from listening to my grandparents and parents talk with each other when I was a little girl. Peppermint Sticks and Banana Peels is the result of listening and watching the people around me.

Best Wishes

Garnette Camp - To a loving mother, grandmother and great grandmother

Betty Ingram   9-19-06

Table of Contents

Courage to Continue 1

Black Diamond Memories 25

She Bloomed Where She Was Planted 27

C.O.D. With Love "Daughter #4" 29

Numbers Game 31

Stockings on the Steps 34

Farewell to a Faithful Friend "In Tune with Our Piano" ... 35

Five Knights and a Princess 36

King Ceilidh 38

"Skinny Simmie" 40

Computer Basics-101 "Senior Style" 88

Writers By the Lakes 90

Sweet Sixteen 92

Grandma's Summer Camp 96

Wanted 9-5 Job, Retirement is Too Exhausting 108

A Cherished Moment 117

Happy Birthday to Me 119

Peppermint Sticks and Banana Peels 121

Courage to Continue

There was a chill in the air as Hannah gathered the wash from the line in the yard. Dark grey clouds moved slowly across the sky and threatened to deposit the first snow of the season on the quiet little town of Smithy.

Hannah lived near the edge of town with her five-year-old twins, Jimmy and Janie. Tom, her husband, had joined a local group that had gone to help the Union forces two years ago. They left in high spirits promising the people of Smithy they would be back soon. They said it wouldn't take long to whip those low down Rebels.

Hannah hadn't heard from Tom for several months and didn't know where he was now. Her parents, brothers and sisters lived twenty miles away and seldom came to visit. Tom had lost both his parents and baby sister during a smallpox epidemic several years ago, leaving Hannah to find support from the community.

The next day Hannah had gotten up early and was ready to hitch their horse Romy to the wagon as the sun began to rise. The twins were running about and yelling at each other about who got to ride next to their mother. She had told them that one could have the favorite seat going and the other could sit next to her on the way home. Jimmy and Janie had both asked many times if they cold go to Miss Sara and Miss Ellen's store while they were in town. Jimmy had even promised not to pull Janie's pigtails anymore, if their mother would take them.

Hannah looked at her mischievous little boy and said, "I'll think about it, but first we have to stop at the general

1

store and get corn for the chickens and feed for Bossy, if we expect her to continue to give milk. The grass in the pasture is gone until next spring."

Jimmy and Janie chattered and giggled as Romy pulled the wagon along. A stop at Sara and Ellen's store was the highlight of the outing for the three of them. Hannah traded butter and eggs for flour and meal. She had not raised a corn patch since Tom went off to war.

Most of their food supply was stored in the cellar and smoke house. Big stone jars of pickled vegetables lined the walls of the cellar and dried beans and apples hung from rafters in the smokehouse. Hannah's parents brought cured ham and bacon when they came to visit at Christmas time.

When Hannah finished at the general store, she loaded the wagon and the twins scampered to their seats. She drove the wagon down the street and turned at the next corner. Janie clapped her hands and said, "Mommy, I smell Miss Sara's Store." Jimmy pointed and said, "I see the big board with the letters on it." Over the door of the building a sign had been painted that said, *"Sara and Ellen's Bake Shop."* Hannah reined Romy into the hitching rail near the store and the three of them were soon greeted by Sara and Ellen. A sign in the front window said. *"Try our Twin Spice Cookies."*

She thought about the circumstances that had brought a bakery to Smithy. Sara and her family had been part of a wagon train that was on the way to the gold fields of California when they were attack by Indians. Hannah remembers when she first heard the sisters tell the story shortly after they arrived in Smithy.

The wagon master gave the signal for the wagons to form a circle. The scout had seen a raiding party riding toward the wagons. Sara's husband grabbed his rifle and took their ten-year-old son to join the other men around the circle.

Flaming arrows were flying through the air and one hit the canvas top of their wagon. The smoke was getting thick and Ellen began to cough and choke, as she was desperately gathering things in the wagon. Sara could not make her understand they had no time to rescue possessions. They had to get out. While the Indians on horses were whooping and the wagon master was yelling orders, Sara jerked on her sister's arm and pushed her out the back of the wagon. They ran to a nearby bush and rolled down a small bank behind the bush. They landed in a ditch out of sight of the wagons.

Sara and Ellen had cautiously crept from their hiding place, after everything became quiet. Little could be found after the raid. Sara's knees became weak as the ground seemed to come up to meet her. Bodies were scattered around the circle that had been formed by the wagons when they first heard the raiding party coming. As she glanced to her right, she saw her ten-year-old son, Jacob lying across the chest of his father. Both had been scalped. Her legs felt numb and her feet seemed to be planted to the ground. She was starring straight ahead. Ellen took her by the arm and said "Sara, we have to get away from here. I've heard that they always come back." Most of the supplies had been taken or destroyed, but they decided to take a quick look before they moved on.

All the horses had been unhitched and stolen except one that had been tied to the last wagon. It had become frightened at the height of the raid and had broken loose while trying to escape from the noise and fire.

While Ellen had gotten the horse that was grazing near by, Sara began to gather things in a sack she had found in a stone jar. Ellen took her apron off and started to search for things. Hot water came up in her throat and a heavy feeling lay in the middle of her chest as she watched her sister move from wagon to wagon. Sara's eyes were fixed and her mouth was drawn in a thin hard line.

Ellen grabbed Sara and shoved her behind a rain barrel as they heard a shrill war hoop in the distance. It seemed to come from behind a hill to their right. As they clung to each other, the frightening looks in Sara's eyes told Ellen that they needed to move quickly. She shook her sister and said, "I'll lead the horse and you stay close by me. We better start walking before the raiders decide to come back."

Sara tied Ellen's apron strings together and with the loose ends of the strings she tied the top of the sack closed and laid the bundle across the back of the horse. Sara had heard the wagon master say that morning that they were near the town of Smithy and should be able to make camp there by evening. She reasoned that if they followed the tracks of the wagons that had gone before them, and the Indians didn't come back, they should be there in a couple of days.

They walked all night stopping only long enough to let the horse drink as they passed by a stream. Sara looked in her sack hoping to find something they could eat, but the raiders had left very little.

She had thrown in a small baby quilt, a half-burned candle, a gourd water dipper, a book of poetry by Robert Browning, a black, well-worn bible and four small cloth bags in a tin box that smelled like cinnamon. Ellen untied her apron and smiled at what she saw. She had hurriedly taken a wooden spoon, three tin plates, a man's shirt from a trunk and a piece of calico that someone had probably planned to use to make a dress. She said to Sara, "I don't see anything to eat." As she began to tie the apron into a bundle, she saw something sticking from the pocket. She pulled out several pieces of beef jerky and even though it wasn't the favorite food of either woman, it looked good to them.

The sun was sinking near the horizon the next evening when Sara saw a speck up ahead. As they continued to walk, she squinted and said, "Ellen, I think I see a church steeple." "Sister, I see it. We must be near the town." As they continued to walk, they saw the tops of other buildings.

They were happy that the first place they came to was the church. It seemed like a safe place to stop. As they approached the building, they noticed a log cabin to the right and back of the white church. Ellen stayed with the horse and Sara walked to the front door and knocked "Hello, anyone here?" When there was no response, she turned to leave and saw a tall man with red hair coming around the corner of the church. He said, "Good morning ladies, I'm Pastor McColly. Can I help you?"

Sara stepped forward and said, "I'm Sara Mitchell and this is my sister, Ellen Brown, and yes, we need help" Maliki McColly looked from one woman to the other and could see that their torn and dirty clothing did not match the manner in which Sara had spoken. He walked to Ellen and said, "Ma'am, may I take your horse? I want you ladies to come around back and meet my wife, Coleen. You can tell her your problem and how we can help. I'll join you as soon as I tend to your horse."

A petite young woman stood on the porch as the three of them walked to the house. Her black hair was neatly pinned in a bun at the nape of her neck. And ringlets fell around her face. Her smile and the sparkle of her grey-green eyes seemed to say welcome. Maliki said, "Coleen, this is Sara Mitchell and her sister, Ellen Brown. They have a problem and maybe we can help."

When they were seated in the front room of the modest cottage, Ellen began to tell their story. Sara's eye misted and tears flowed down her cheeks when Ellen told how Sara had last seen her husband and son.

When Ellen had finished the story, Coleen took charge and said, "Maliki, you should go talk with the sheriff while I see what I can do for Sara and Ellen. Ladies, come with me." They followed her to the kitchen where she asked them to sit at the table. They soon had cold biscuits, apple butter, thick slices of ham, and tall glasses of milk that had been brought from the cellar and placed in front of them. The sisters hadn't realized how hungry they were or how much they had missed eating in a real kitchen until now.

Coleen had found some clean clothing from the mission barrel that had been sent to the church from the wealthy father of John the local general store owner. The clothing usually arrived from Boston twice a year. John gave the job to Maliki of passing out the clothing to the needy. She sent Sara and Ellen to the extra bedroom that she used for a sewing room with a pan of water and told them to come back to the kitchen when they had changed.

Maliki had returned and was sitting at the table when they came from the sewing room. He began telling them about his talk with the sheriff. A posse was being gathered and the sheriff planned to ride out to the wagon site and see if anything of value could be found and if the raiders had been back. When the front door opened and someone yelled, "Anybody home?" Coleen called, "Come on in Bertha we're in the kitchen" as she got up from the table to greet her friend. Bertha looked surprised as she saw the strangers sitting at the table.

Smithy was a small town and new people drew the attention of everyone. Coleen said, "Bertha I would like you to meet Sara Mitchell and her sister, Ellen Brown. They have had some trouble and Maliki and I are trying to figure out what we can do to help." As was the custom in Smithy, when people dropped in at the preacher's house, they made themselves at home.

Bertha was soon seated at the table with the others. She was a short middle aged lady with a ready smile. She looked from Sara to Ellen and said, "Honey, tell Bertha what's bothering you. It can't be all that bad." Coleen could see the apprehension in the faces of the two sisters. Sara's eyes began to mist and Ellen drew her mouth in a tight hard line and her chin began to quiver. Coleen put her arm around Sara's shoulder and said, "Would you like me to tell Bertha your story?" With a sense of relief, both women nodded yes. Sara and Ellen could feel the compassion in Coleen's voice and was thankful that she left out some of the gruesome details of the horrible time they had experienced.

Bertha was known for her caring and loving help when anyone was in need in the community. She was a widow whose husband had died at the beginning of the war.

She wiped the tears away and as always was a woman of action. "Why don't you ladies come to my house and stay for a while until we can figure out what to do?" Coleen said, "She lives close and Maliki and I can care for your horse and see you often."

Maliki rose from his chair and said, "I'll spread the word that we will have a meeting after church Sunday. We will get some ideas that might help and everyone knows that a meeting after preaching service means that the ladies will bring their favorite dishes for a delicious meal."

Sara and Ellen were quiet as they went with Bertha. They didn't know what to expect but were grateful they would have a place to be in out of the weather that night. Bertha was the town's seamstress. She had started sewing for people as a means of supporting herself after the death of her husband. As she pushed the door open, Bertha said with a chuckle, "Come on in girls, It isn't very big, but we will manage just fine."

They entered a large room and could see an area that had been added on in the back that held a wood burning cooking stove and some shelves had been built against the wall. One corner held sewing things and a bed. In the center of the room were Bertha's pride and joy, a round table with claw feet and two matching chairs that she had brought with her when she came west years ago. It had been a wedding gift from her grandmother.

The next morning, Sara asked Bertha what they could do to help. Bertha knew they wanted to feel useful and said, "How would you like to cook something for the church dinner tomorrow? That would give me time to catch up on some of my sewing." Ellen asked, "What do you want cooked?" "Whatever you like, just look in the cellar and in the cupboard and see what we have." Sara thought about the spices that they had brought with them and asked Bertha if she would like her to bake a cake. Ellen spoke up and said, "Sara bakes a cake that was a favorite of everyone back home."

Maliki stopped by that evening to give a report to the ladies about the sheriff's findings. A posse of five men had volunteered to go with him. He said they knew they were near the site of the Indian raid when the odor of burning wood was in the air. As they rode past a large boulder in a turn on the trail, the reality of what the women had told them was evident. They found no bodies of women only small children and men. The women had probably been taken back to the Indian village to be used as slaves.

The posse dug a large grave and buried all the bodies together. One of the men had lashed a cross together and another carved the date on a board. They placed these on the grave. As the men removed their hats and bowed their heads, Deacon Brown said a prayer. The sheriff and the men spread out and began to look around the wagons. The raiders had apparently come back and taken all the tools, food or anything of value. The posse found only a few books. They put them in their saddle bags and decided that Sara and Ellen might want to share them with Miss Meg, the school teacher at Smithy.

The sun was shining brightly the next morning as the three women started to walk to the church. Each one carried a wicker basket loaded with food. Bertha introduced the sisters to the people that were gathered outside the church. Word of their story had spread quickly since they arrived in town. Preacher McColly explained their problem for the benefit of those who might have missed the news. He said, "We will discuss this during the dinner at the close of the service."

Hannah never complained, but after she tucked the twins in at night, she was lonely. She often longed to have someone to talk with, someone to share her hopes and plans for the future. She decided to offer her home to Sara and Ellen. She approached Maliki as he stood by the door greeting people and asked, "Do you think Sara and Ellen would like to stay with me and the children for a while?" Maliki smiled and said, "That is such a kind offer. So many people have come forth as good Christians willing to open their homes to these two ladies in need." The minister had asked anyone that had a suggestion to come and tell him because the sisters didn't know anyone. Maliki thought they might be overwhelmed, if they were asked to make a decision. Several families had offered to take them in, including Hannah. While people were visiting and eating he called his wife aside and told her of the help that people had offered. After considering all the options, they both decided that Hannah's offer would be best for the sisters. It would be a help to Hannah and she had a barn for their horse.

Coleen was pleased that Sara and Ellen trusted her and her husband to make a decision for them. She asked the three women to step inside the church where they could talk quietly. After a brief discussion, it was decided that Sara and Ellen would go home that day with Hannah.

Coleen left the three women talking and slipped out to tell Maliki what had been decided. He moved to the church steps and when he had the attention of the crowd, he told them that God had provided for our new friends and they would be going home with Hannah and the twins. He said, "I want to thank all of you for your concern and offers of help, and I ask that you pray for God's guidance to show you what we can do to help these ladies face the future and deal with the tragedy they had experienced."

Life for the sisters was changing so quickly. They had been a help to Hannah since she brought them home after the church dinner. Ellen tended the garden and cared for the farm animals and Sara adapted to the cooking and other duties in the house. They were both thankful for Hannah's kindness and the twins were a delight to be around. Hannah was glad for their help with the chores but she cherished the time she had to talk with adults. They were adjusting to living with Hannah but knew they needed to find a way to make enough money to support them.

Sara and Ellen had been with them about a month when Pastor McColly came to visit. Maliki listened as Sara told him their concern about earning money. He promised he would think about it and talk with them on Sunday when they came to church. The twins liked the bedtime stories that

Sara told them. She remembered the favorite of her son, Jacob, when he was their age. He never seemed to tire of hearing about Joseph, the carpenter and his son, Jesus. It was at times like these that reminded Sara that she would never be able to read to her son and hold him close again. Somehow, seeing the delight in the twins' faces helped to ease the pain.

Ellen mostly worked outside but she liked to bake a special cookie. She rolled dough and cut it into pieces the shape of a boy and a girl. Jimmy and Janie named the new treat, Aunt Ellen's Twin Cookies.

Hannah had encouraged her children to call Ellen and Sara Aunt. They seldom saw her family and this seemed the best names for their new friends.

Maliki asked Sara, Ellen and Hannah to stop by the parsonage after church. He said Coleen would fix dinner and they would have a chance to talk. After the twins had eaten and were playing in the yard, Coleen said, "Maliki took my idea to the church deacons and they agreed to loan you money to buy ingredients to bake cookies and cakes."

They could be offered to people that come through town with the wagon trains. Bertha said she would be glad for you to bring what you baked to her house. Some of the other people said they would help by talking with the wagon master about the baked goods. Ellen said, "Sara, don't you think we should give some of what we earn to Hannah and Bertha for the use of their kitchens?" Bertha raised her hands in a sweeping motion and said, "Land sakes alive, I wouldn't hear of such a thing. The people of Smithy gave me a helping hand after I lost my husband and was trying to start my sewing business." Coleen said, "I think Bertha is right. God put us on this earth to watch out for each other and that is what the people of Smithy do." A few days later Maliki and

Coleen went to the general store and bought what Coleen thought would be needed for Sara and Ellen to start their new business. They stopped at Hannah's house one afternoon while they were calling on other church families. Sara had been eager to get started but hesitated to ask Hannah to make an extra trip to town. When Coleen showed them what she had selected, they smiled and both sisters tried to hug her at the same time. Maliki gave Sara what money was left from the amount that the church deacons had given him for the sisters. Ellen said, "Thank you, pastor. We'll use this to buy butter, eggs and milk from Hannah."

The wagon train had stopped for the evening, when the wagon master said, "Folks, Wendell has some news." A tall young man stepped near the middle of the circle and said, "I've scouted ahead to the town of Smithy, which we will reach tomorrow afternoon. You will be able to fill your water barrels and get what supplies you need from the general store.

There is a special treat for those who might be interested. Baked goods will be for sale. I don't want to frighten you, but before you make up your mind about buying cakes and pies, I have a story to tell you why a small town like Smithy has a business like this. He knew they were near where the massacre had occurred. He told the group the story of the Indian raid and what Sara and Ellen were trying to do to start a new life. He heard sobs from the crowd as he talked. Finally in a husky voice he said, "I plan to do what I can to help."

The first day of Sara and Ellen's sale went well. The people had been on the trail for a long time. The freshly baked cakes and pies reminded them of the homes they had left behind when they joined the wagon train to go west.

Word soon spread that the town of Smithy had something special to offer. The stage coach passengers were buying a piece of cake or cookies to take with them to the next stop. The ginger cookies that Jimmy and Janie called "The Twin Cookies" were the favorite of all the children.

The hellish war had finally ended and Tom was on his way home. As he rode along, he looked at his old army buddy with a grin and said, "It won't be much longer. We should be in Smithy this time tomorrow. Hannah will be surprised and the kids might not know me."

Jonas with a questioning look asked "What is Smithy like?" Tom thoughtfully looked at him and said, "Where do I start? I have lived there since I was four years old. My parents sold their home in Virginia. They had dreams of starting a new life on the frontier out west. They were young and looking for adventure. When they joined the wagon train, my dad told the wagon master he was looking for a town that needed a blacksmith. As they came near Smithy, the wagon scout said to dad, "Smithy might be what you are looking for. They don't have a blacksmith and the Crystal River a few miles north of town has the best fishing you could ever imagine. Homesteader farms are near. They have horses that need shoes and I'm sure that a stagecoach team horse might lose a shoe sometimes."

"Smithy with its dusty main street and board walks is one of God's greatest creations." Jonas smiled and said. "You sure make it sound good." "Partner, we have everything a man could want. There is a general store, saloon, school, church, and a woman even has a sewing business. All of that besides the blacksmith shop that Dad started."

"What will your wife think of you bringing a stranger home with you?" "Now don't worry, Jonas. We have an extra room and when I tell Hannah we have been buddies all thru the war and that you took a bullet for me. She'll be happy to meet you." Jonas shook his head and said, "Naw, Tom. I didn't do anything. I just happened to shove you down, and a 'Johnny Reb's' aim hit my leg, instead of your back."

Jonas had never married. His parents and sister had died in the diphtheria epidemic before he joined up with the Union Army. The only family he had was some cousins that had gone to the California gold fields a few years ago. Tom had convinced him that Smithy would be a good place to settle down.

Jimmy ran into the kitchen and said, "Mommy, I see two horses coming down the road." Hannah folded the dishcloth and hung it on the rack near the back door. She had finished the supper dishes while Sara and Ellen went to the barn to milk the cow and gather the eggs.

Hannah looked out the window and saw two horses. As they came nearer, she thought she saw two men, but she couldn't make out who they were. Who could be coming at this hour of the day?

Jonas said, "Tom, you ride on and I'll wait here under this oak tree until you see your family and tell them about me." Tom nodded and continued on down the road. His heart was racing as he approached the house. He had thought about this moment many times during the long evenings and nights in the encampment.

Hannah stood frozen and leaned against the porch post. Were her eyes playing tricks on her, or was that Tom she saw dismount and come running toward her? His shirt hung loosely from his shoulders. His sunken eyes and prominent cheek bones told her instantly that he had been through some hard times. There was no doubt, when Hannah saw that lopsided grin that her Tom had come back to her.

She wrapped her arms around him and knew that God had answered her prayers.

Jimmy and Janie stood in the yard and looked at their mother and knew something good was happening. She was crying and smiling at the same time. Could this man she called Tom be their dad? Their mom had told them he was away at war, fighting to make all people free and someday he would come home to them. Two years is a long time in the life of a five-year-old and the twins didn't remember much about their father.

Tom looked at Hannah with a gleam in his eye and asked, "Who are this young man and lady? He wanted to grab and hug both his children at the same time, but he was afraid of frightening them. They looked puzzled and stood holding hands. Hannah walked toward them and said, Children come and say hello to your dad. We have talked about him coming home and now he is here." As the twins moved toward him he stooped down and opened his arms, he was amazed at how much Janie resembled her mother and could see that Jimmy looked like him when he was a boy. He held them close as he looked at Hannah and said, "We need to talk."

As they sat on the porch steps, he told her about Jonas. "I hope you don't mind that I brought him home with me." "Tom, I would be happy to meet the man that saved your life. I have news that you should know." Before she could say anything else, Sara called from the kitchen and said, "Hannah I got nine eggs this evening and Ellen is putting the milk in the cellar." Tom looked at Hannah puzzled. She got up and said, "I'll be right back." She went to the kitchen and told Sara and Ellen that Tom had come home and she wanted to talk with him for a little while. "Sure Hannah, Ellen and I will be out back when you need us."

Hannah went back to the front porch and began to tell Tom of the Indian raid and how the community was trying to help Sara and Ellen start a new life. Tom said, "I'll get Jonas and we will all get to know each other at the same time."

The group talked long after the sun went down. Both men had gazed in wonder at the food that was placed on the table for them. The women said it was just what was left over from supper. Ellen went about warming the fodder beans that had bits of pork cooked in them and the boiled potatoes. Sara went to the cellar and brought fresh milk and butter while Hannah set the applesauce and cornbread on the table. Ellen insisted that the spice cake that had been baked for the sale tomorrow should be cut as a welcome home treat for the two men.

It was decided that Jonas would sleep in the barn that night. They would have time to make plans tomorrow.

The next few days were spent in Tom getting acquainted with Jimmy and Janie. He was proud of how well his wife had kept their home while he was away.

Jonas had a noticeable limp, but he never complained and was able to help in the garden and repair some fence before he went to Smithy to look for work.

Sara and Ellen had been thinking about finding some place in town for their business because they had outgrown Hannah's kitchen. They talked with Coleen and Maliki the next Sunday after church about their wish. They said they would ask around and see what might be available.

One afternoon a few days later, Coleen and Bertha had come to visit. They had driven Bertha's buggy and were excited about what they had to tell Sara and Ellen. Isaac. Simm's was moving his feed store to a bigger place and his old store would be for rent. Bertha said, "It would be perfect with a little fixin' up." Coleen said, "It is big enough to make a kitchen, bedroom and a room to display the baked goods."

Sara and Ellen sat and listened as their two friends continued to talk about what could be done. Finally they paused and Coleen said, "Well girls, how does it sound?" Sara looked at her sister and said, "Ellen, do you think we could do it? I would be glad to clean but I don't know much about using a saw or hammer. I know we would need shelves."

Jonas had been standing near by and heard the last of the conversation. He walked to the group and said, "Ladies, I've done some carpenter work in my time and I'd be glad to help out."

In the weeks that followed the sisters were busy with their new project. Sara continued to bake in Hannah's kitchen and took the cakes and cookies to Bertha's house to sell. Ellen scrubbed the walls of the old feed store while Jonas made new shelves and drove nails into the back wall to hang clothes on. Maliki and some of the men had made a table and found a couple extra chairs from the church congregation. The most important item for the new business was a cast-iron stove that John would have to send for and wait for the supply wagon to bring. He had offered to wait until their business got started for payment for the stove. Until then Sara and Ellen would cook outside in the back of the building using the skills they had learned while on the wagon train. They would use Bertha's kitchen to do the baking because it was near.

Coleen invited Sara, Ellen, Mary, Bertha and Jonas to her house one afternoon. She thought it would be nice for them to get together and talk about the finishing touches of the store Jonas smiled at Coleen and said, "You ladies pick what you want. I'm no good at making things pretty. The only thing I ever painted was a barn. Give me a holler when you decide and I'll be there to help."

As they sat around Coleen's kitchen table drinking tea, the five women felt excited. Bertha said, "As soon as we decide on the paint for the walls, I'll stitch up a curtain for the front window and a divider to put across the section that will be the bedroom. Come on girls, think. I can't wait to get started." Coleen's eyes sparkled as she looked from Sara to Ellen and said, "What is your favorite color? Sara looked thoughtfully and said, "Back home we had cream-colored heavy paper on the walls except the kitchen had Jenny Lind boards on it. Ellen smiled and asked Coleen where they would get the paint. Coleen thought of Ellen's practicality as she answered, "John at the general store keeps some on hand. He buys it when the supply wagon comes thru town."

Coleen noticed Hannah had been quiet. Hannah you look like you have wheels turning in your head with an idea. "Well," Hannah said, "I was thinking we could use white paint. It would look clean and Bertha's curtains would add a touch of color. Sara said, "Ellen, why don't we give Bertha the piece of blue calico we brought from the wagon train to use for the curtains?" Ellen nodded and said, "That is a great idea." Hannah said, "I think when people get a whiff of the ginger cookies, they won't notice much of anything else.

Sara liked the idea of using white paint. It reminded her of the lily of the valley flowers that were planted around her house that she left to come west. She smiled as she thought of meeting Silas at a barn dance and the beautiful wedding that her mother had planned for her two years later.

Sara was awakened from her daydreaming by a question from Bertha, "Sara, does that sound good to you?" "It sure does." They talked awhile and then everyone agreed they had a plan and were anxious to get started.

Jonas had told the women he would stop by the general store and check on the stove that John had ordered. He had been going about town trying to get acquainted with the people of Smithy. "He was starting to like it here."

He wondered what he could do to make a living. Being a ranch hand before his army days as a foot soldier was all he knew. The pain from the injury to his leg was bad at times. He realized a ranch owner wouldn't want to hire a man that didn't feel up to working all the time.

His mother had made sure he went to the little one room school near their house when he was a boy. His dad didn't see any need of it. He hadn't been to school and he made a living on the farm. Jonas was proud of his mother's ability to read and write, and glad she had made it a priority for him.

He was lost in thought as he rode along the lane toward Tom and Hannah's farm. "I can read, write, do figures, and I like being around people. Maybe John at the general store could use some help. I'll see him first thing in the morning after I pick the beans in the garden. I heard Hannah say she wanted to pickle them in a big stone jar."

When Jonas entered the store the next day, he saw men gathered around the pot belly stove in the center of the room. Cane back chairs had been placed in a circle and John said, "Jonas come and have a seat. Have you decided what you are going to do yet?" "I would like to stay in Smithy if I could find a job." As he leaned back on his chair, John said, "I might be able to help. I need a man since Seth left for the gold fields. I couldn't pay much, but you could bunk in the back room where I store extra things." John knew that Jonas had been sleeping in Tom's barn. Jonas said, "That sounds fine with me. When can I start?" John extended his hand as he turned toward Jonas and said, "I'll see you here Monday morning. I'm usually here by six o'clock."

John had left his home in Boston in 1849 when news of the discovery of gold in California had filtered back East. His idea of getting rich in the gold fields had changed when the stagecoach stopped in Smithy and he met the local parson's daughter.

He took the money that his parents had given him for a grubstake and bought the general store. The owner was getting on in years and his rheumatism bothered him. He didn't want to admit to his wife that on a rainy day he hurt all over and it was hard for him to get around.

John's parents had dreamed of their only son studying law with his father, but he was restless and talked of nothing else but going West. They wanted him to be happy and had wished him well when he left. He had not regretted his decision to settle in Smithy and his wife and children made his life complete

He liked to talk with the local people when they came in the store. He especially liked to hear the news from back East when the wagon trains and stage coaches stopped.

Through the years his parents had visited twice and he had taken his wife and children to Boston for his sister's wedding.

Jonas hadn't dreamed of getting a job that easily and he couldn't wait to tell Tom the good news that he would be able to stay in Smithy.

Ellen was pulling weeds in the garden when he rode up. She waved and said, "We got the paint and plan to work at the building in the morning." Jonas waved back and said "I'll be there."

At supper that evening he told Tom about his job and that he could help Sara and Ellen tomorrow because he didn't start until Monday morning.

Before a week had past, most of the people in town and nearby farms had been to see Sara and Ellen's new home and business. The women marveled at the bright blue curtains at the front window and the darker blue material that hung on a rope to separate the bedroom from the rest of the store.

Sara and Ellen soon realized if they were to keep their customers happy they would need to have gingerbread cookies on hand at all times. Word spread from one stagecoach stop to the next, that the stop at Smithy had a bakery and sold ginger cookies that were delicious. Wendell told the wagon masters in St. Louis and his other scout friends to watch for the town of Smithy along the trail.

They had used up the spices that they had carried with them after the Indian raid and John had very little left in his store. Jonas admired both women for the way they were working to put their lives back together. He knew they seldom left the bakery except when they went to church on Sunday.

He couldn't describe his feelings for Ellen when she smiled at him. His heart beat faster and the sparkle of her deep blue eyes made his stomach do flip flops. It was a bright day when he got to sit in the pew with Ellen and Sara on Sunday morning. He hoped that Ellen would soon show signs of caring for him.

He wanted to do something to help. He shared his concern with John of the possibility of the sisters not having the spices for baking that had made Smithy a favorite stop of people on the wagon train and the stagecoach passengers.

John said, "Jonas, don't worry. I'll write to dad and tell him about Sara and Ellen's bakery and how they are trying to start a new life. He has friends in the import business and their ships land in Boston after making trips to the Far East. It will take a while, but once we get started, keeping a supply of spices won't be a problem."

John continued, "While we're waiting, I'll ask Wendell and some of the other scouts to see what is available in St. Louis. In the mean time, why don't you dig sassafras roots for the ladies to make tea. They could sell it to the people to have with their cookies."

Jonas was excited with the idea that he could do something to help. He wanted the sisters' business to do well.

Coleen and her friend Meg, who taught school in the one room school at the edge of town, decided they wanted to do something extra nice for their new friends. They thought of all the things the community had done and wanted to do something different. Meg jumped up from the table where she and Coleen had been talking and said, "I know, let's make a sign and put it on the front of the building." "Oh Meg, that is a great idea." They immediately began to plan. How big would it be? Would Maliki help them cut the board? What color would the letters be? They talked for a while and finally realized they would have to decide what it would say. It was finally agreed that *Sara and Ellen's Bake Shop* would be perfect.

Many people in the small town knew that Ellen and Jonas were fond of each other and they were hoping that a wedding was in the future. Meg and Susan thought if they put Sara's name on the sign that it would help ease the pain that she continued to feel about the loss of her husband and son.

They decided to work in a small building that Maliki used to store tools. The women wanted the sign to be a surprise. On a pleasant Saturday morning, the sun was shining as a small group gathered at the parsonage. They planned to take the sign to the bakery and let Sara and Ellen decide how they wanted it to be placed on the building. Jonas carried it and Tom brought a ladder. Maliki had a hammer and nails in his toolbox. Meg, Coleen and Hannah walked along with Jimmy and Janie.

When they arrived, Meg went in first and asked Sara and Ellen to come outside and meet some friends of hers. As they came out the front door, the twins yelled, "Surprise!" They were jumping around and both talking at the same time. "Look what we brought." Tears rolled down Sara's cheeks. She didn't say anything as she ran from one to the other hugging everyone. She knelt down and embraced the children and finally said, "I love you."

Ellen had been thanking everyone and asking questions. "Whose idea was it? It is just beautiful." When things quieted down some, the men put the sign over the front door. Sara thought more people would notice it there while they were walking or riding down the street When Sara saw the sign hanging over the door, with their names on it she realized that she and Ellen were moving to a new phase of their lives.

Sara stood at the front of the little white church beside her sister. Her thoughts drifted back over the past two years. Today Ellen wore a wedding dress that was a gift from Bertha and Hannah. They said making the dress was a labor of love and refused to be paid.

The sun light filtered through the window and seemed to add an aura of peace and tranquility around Ellen and Jonas as they stood before Maliki ready to repeat their wedding vows. Tom stood by his old army buddy that had saved his life during the war and thought, "I want him to find the happiness that I have with my Hannah."

While Maliki prayed Sara thought, "Our bakery business has thrived and God has blessed us with many friends. When I came to Smithy, my heart was burdened and I could think of nothing else except Ellen and I were all alone."

The horror of the nightmares of the Indian raid had lessened with time, and even though they would always be with her, she was able to savor the happy memories she had with her dear husband and son.

As Meg sang the words of the song *Barbara Ellen* in her sweet contralto voice, a feeling of peace embraced Sara and she knew that God had a plan for her life in Smithy. She joined the celebration of the happy gathering as Maliki said, "Jonas and Ellen, I now pronounce you man and wife."

Black Diamond Memories

Luther slowly came up the lane that lead to his childhood home. The days of the Great Depression have come and gone but memories of the past are with him. As he looks ahead, he is aware of a majestic throne of black diamonds near a tall grey house that seems to stand guard over its surroundings.

He remembers pleasant times of long ago. The antics of the Katzenjammer Kids and the strength of Popeye after gulping spinach are vivid in his memory.

His mother would gather him with his brothers and sisters around her rocking chair by the black cast iron stove as she read the funny papers to them. The stove had been feed with the black jewels and sent warmth around the room. He savored the cozy feeling he had as the stove sometimes changed its color from black to red.

The bucket that sat by the stove cried out to be filled. As he became older, it was his job to keep it full. With the encouragement of his Mother, he did his job. He would have much rather been riding circles around the big black pile in the yard on his bicycle. When he thought his mother wasn't looking, he liked to jump over the lumps that had strayed from the pile.

The small boy looked forward to the day the big truck came up the road to empty its load of shiny black lumps on the dwindling pile. He dreamed of the day that he could gun the engine of a big truck. His eyes looked in wonder as the lever was pulled and the bed of the truck tilted and spilled its load.

Sometimes his father brought a few sacks of coal home in the family car, but that was of little interest to the small boy. The car was quiet and the wheels didn't spin in the gravel like the big truck.

The father who brought sacks of coal and the mother who read to her children are no longer with him. The little ones who followed the adventures of Popeye and Olyve Oyle are now grandparents.

The black diamond throne has dwindled and the big trucks can no longer be seen on the lane that leads to the tall grey house that has stood like a guardian angel over its surroundings for so many years.

The annual gathering of this family and the memories they share helps to keep this a place of beauty for future generations to cherish.

She Bloomed Where She Was Planted

I often think of one of the most incredible ladies I have ever met. Yula Ingram was a part of my life from the time I married her son in 1950 until her death at the age of 88 in 1992. Yula was the mother of five boys and three girls, and raised them on a farm in the hills of West Virginia. Over the years, she was also blessed with 23 grandchildren.

Yula remembered everyone on their birthdays and Christmas with homemade gifts. The family treasured the crocheted doilies and dresser scarves edged with intricate lace that she made. She also sewed crazy quilts that were knotted with colorful thread. The tissue wrapping paper around the gifts was always secured with ribbons and yarn, but amazingly no scotch tape. The grandchildren marveled at that feat.

Yula was soft spoken and steadfastly devoted to her children, and especially to the care of a daughter who was in poor health. One son, who never married, continued to live with his mother and help with the farm chores.

When Yula finished high school in 1922, she took a course at Mountain State Business College. Over the years, she put her typing skills to use and sent my family many letters that had been written on her Royal typewriter. She was an avid reader and especially looked forward to the *Grit* newspaper and *Reader's Digest* arriving in the mail. She enjoyed visiting with family. They gathered around the big, warm, coal stove and discussed current events and the latest escapades of her grandchildren, who often were playing nearby with oatmeal box drums and wooden spool blocks. When her grandchildren got tired of their indoor toys, sometimes Yula would take them to visit the chicken coop to feed the chickens and gather eggs.

After the death of her husband and later a son, who had lived at home, the other children continued to help their mother so she might stay in the house she had called home for sixty years. One of her sons started an apple orchard in the spot that was once called the back garden Yula was particularly fond of apples and made a pot of applesauce every day for as long as anyone could remember.

Spring mornings were some of her favorite times as she watched the morning sun shine on the orchard when it was in full bloom. The humming birds and bees would flit from one pink blossom to another gathering nectar.

Yula always met life with strength and acceptance and was a wonderful role model for all those around her. Like the sweet peas climbing the side of her cellar house and the apple trees in the back garden, Yula truly bloomed where she was planted.

C.O.D. With Love
"Daughter #4"

It seems only a short time since we walked down the hill and turned around the corner to pick up a special delivery for Capehart Street.

The people in the big red building took one look at me and said, "There isn't anything here for the Ingram family."

I insisted there had to be, because I had been getting calls every five minutes for the last hour saying to stop A.S.A.P. to claim the package. When they realized that I refused to leave, the supervisor was called. With a disgusted look, she said, "I'll look in the back where the deliveries are dropped off and see if I can find anything."

We waited and after about two hours she came carrying a bundle wrapped in a pink covering. She said, "The shipping ticket says it is 20 inches long and weighs 7 pounds and 10 ounces. You must have ordered something valuable because it was sent C.O.D. and I need to collect $300.00 for it." We had waited nine months for this package so we whipped out the checkbook and gave the woman what she asked for, no questions asked.

We were delighted when we opened the package and found that it had moving parts and was pleasant to look at. It was one of the best things we ever purchased for our house. We have cherished it through the years and not once did we ever consider giving it to the Salvation Army or sending it to a school rummage sale.

Since that morning on October 19, it has grown in value. I can't imagine what our life would have been like if we had not stood our ground and insisted they check again for our package.

Always stand up for what is rightfully yours. We did and were rewarded with a delightful daughter. We see her as a person with a sense of humor, ambitious and a caring attitude for the people around her. She continues to shed sunshine in our lives and we are proud to be the parents of Jo Ellen who is affectionately known as Daughter #4.

Numbers Game

I opened my eyes as the alarm clock jingled and stared into the dark room. It couldn't be time to get up. I hadn't gotten to bed until past midnight, but I knew I had to be up at 5:00 a.m. and ready to greet three little girls when they came downstairs. They would be eager to see what Santa Claus had left for them.

My plan was to slip down stairs to the kitchen, start the coffee brewing and make hot chocolate. Vic and I would sit and drink coffee and admire the Christmas tree that we had finished decorating a few hours ago.

As I approached the top of the stairs, I sensed something was different. I thought I heard paper rustling. I listened again and all was quiet. Thoughts of a burglar lurking in the dark caused me to awaken Vic. Armed with a small ball bat, we cautiously descended the steps.

The scene that greeted us was beyond belief. Our daughter, seven-year-old Jean sat on the floor and her younger sisters, Vicki and Gayle were close by. Each child had a stack of presents in front of her. A tea set was on a small table and Raggety Ann and Andy were playing host to Barbie. As I was surveying the situation, Jean looked up and said, "Mommy, we didn't want to wake you up." I wasn't thinking straight and the first thing I said was, "How did your sister get out of the baby bed?" With a big grin that showed the space left where she recently had lost a tooth, Jean said, "Vicki and I helped her."

Jean could read and had carefully sorted all the gifts that were under the tree. Other family members would be arriving later that morning and also had packages. Every thing was in place, except what had been tagged for the three little red-headed girls of the Ingram family.

I couldn't let them know my true feelings at the moment. I was proud that Jean could read and that they were resourceful enough to use a flashlight so they wouldn't disturb their parents. I was also glad they had learned to respect other people's property by not opening every present they saw.

I looked at their happy faces and said, "Don't you think we should wait for your grandma and the rest of the family to come?" The girls seemed content to play with the presents that had been opened and to wait for the other people to arrive.

When the children were small, I could shop before Christmas and bring gifts in the house and hide them. I didn't have to worry about them snooping, because I told them if they found anything, I would give it to the Salvation Army toy collection. I also told them they had to help Santa by giving the Salvation Army a used toy for Santa to pick up as he passed by with his sleigh and reindeer.

This "give it to the Salvation Army" ploy lasted for a while, and then I had to face the fact that our little girls were getting smarter every day. The tall tales I had been telling them wouldn't work anymore.

That year a family tradition was started. The following Christmas I assigned a secret number to each child and all the gifts were labeled with numbers instead of names. The secret numbers were not revealed until Christmas morning. This added a touch of mystery to the gifts that were placed under the tree before Christmas.

We adopted a ritual of our daughters waiting upstairs for Grandma and the rest of the family to arrive each Christmas morning. On Christmas Eve, they took the toaster, a loaf of bread, butter, jelly and orange juice to their bedroom and had a breakfast feast while they waited for the Christmas guests the next morning.

They chose to continue the tradition of being referred to as "daughters with numbers." Jean was #1, Vicki #2, Gayle #3 and Kelli, the youngest, was #4.

Many times during their college years I found it difficult to tell which one I was talking with when they called home. The girls found this amusing and would identify themselves by number. I have received many greeting cards through the years with envelopes addressed from daughter # . . . .

This family tradition started because three little girls couldn't wait to see what Santa had left for them. Taking matters into their own hands, they took a flashlight, crept down the stairs, and unwrapped Santa's bounty.

Stockings on the Steps

Bright colored felt socks hang from the stair spindles waiting for Santa to appear. They are proud to be identified by names embroidered across their top. Jingle bells' dangle from their toes.

From their place of honor they reign as royalty over the Christmas activities centered around four little girls. As the family traditions unfold, they anticipate the arrival of the Christmas tree, which each year reaches the ceiling of the room. Soon glittering tensile and brightly colored bulbs will adorn the branches, and later the children will string popcorn and cranberries to add to the decorations, while strains of "Deck the Halls" float around the room.

The presents from Santa are left around the tree un-wrapped. He is much too busy to wrap each one. The ritual of opening presents on Christmas morning starts with the youngest family member and proceeds according to age. Everyone has a chance to see what each person receives. The socks know that the gifts they hold will be opened later. From their position high on the steps, they hear the squeals of joy and see the glow on faces as ribbons are broken and paper is torn from packages.

Through the years, the four socks have welcomed new members to the family. Sixteen socks now hang on the steps.

The socks have many memories tucked away of a family that has shared the joy and love of this special time of year. They hang silently as part of the Christmas decorations. Each sock has a special place in the hearts of the four little girls who first hung them in their place of honor so many years ago.

Farewell to a Faithful Friend
"In Tune with Our Piano"

Melody is the daughter of William and Cynthia Bush Lane. She was born in Chicago, Illinois 1916.

Her life has been devoted to bringing joy to those she served. She joined the Victor Ingram family in December 1975.

The Ingram daughters have left the old house and Melody longs to be in a home with small children again.

When she was invited to move to the home of Taylor and Jennifer, she was overjoyed. She was eager to get to know these young girls. She was sure they would soon be making beautiful music together.

Melody has always been considered the beauty of the Lane children. Her dark flawless complexion and perfect white teeth drew attention from those she met. She refused many suitors and knew she would only be happy creating music to stir man's soul.

Vic and Betty thank her for the years of joy she brought to their family and wish her well in her new adventure.

Five Knights and a Princess

Grandmothers are known for many things. They bake cookies and love to hold little ones on their knee and make them feel like they are the greatest creation since God set Adam and Eve in the Garden of Eden.

My greatest talent as a grandmother is expounding the virtues of six perfect children that my daughters have trusted me to call grandchildren. I have practiced restraint through the years and seldom embarrass my family as I rant and rave about the accomplishments of my grandchildren.

Twenty years ago I joined a grandparent's club called, "Dial for Details." It is composed of people who have grandchildren that live too far away to visit often. We keep in-touch by using the telephone and when we are feeling low we dial another lonely grandparent and cry on each other's shoulder. We can also vent our frustration and anger when one of the neighbors makes a statement like, "I haven't seen Emily or Shawn for two weeks."

As technology advanced, I added email as a resource to keep up with the happenings of this special group of people.

Elizabeth, as you approach your 15th birthday, I look to the past and see a beautiful baby girl. Later as a toddler that shy smile became a part of you.

Due to the generosity of your parents, I have seven framed pictures of you on one wall in my home. Many more are displayed in albums.

After retirement I became interested in the computer. I remember one of my first lessons was when I was visiting in Maryland and you taught me to play Solitaire. You were so kind and patient as you worked with a novice. Our roles were reversed. I was the child and you were the adult five-year-old.

Your recent award in the state science competition confirms my belief that you have the ability to reach for the stars. Your love of reading has broadened your interest in the things around you and the gift of expressing your feelings through art should be cherished.

I would like to write a fairy tale for children about five knights in shining armor defending the kingdom of Bowdoinham where Princess Elizabeth lives with her parents, King Paul and Queen Jean.

The Princess would be adorned with precious jewels. Her favorite would be a necklace of brilliant rubies depicting the month of her birth.

Elizabeth, if the wheels in my head can turn to create a story of the beautiful princess, the kingdom of Bowdoinham is at your command.

The world is waiting to see which direction you take in the future. As one of your loyal subjects, I wish the Princess of Bowdoinham a Happy Birthday.

Grandma Betty

King Ceilidh

A long time ago in the faraway land of Vergen lived King Ceilidh. He was young and had not chosen a bride. Maidens from every part of the kingdom dreamed of becoming queen. The young king had black wavy hair, dark expressive eyes, and his smile seemed to say he was a happy person.

He could often be seen with the serfs that cared for the palace grounds. He was adamant about keeping the lawn free of crabgrass. He would pull up clumps and shake them with gusto until not a trace of dirt could be found on the roots. He enjoyed wearing the necklace that was engraved with the family crest as he surveyed the perimeter of his domain.

He ruled his people with a firm hand and was fair in the decisions he made. His subjects were loyal and strived to do his will. The lowly scullery maids were happy when they were assigned by the head cook, Kelo, to bake his favorite biscuits.

Ceilidh had fond memories of his childhood. He seldom had trouble with his nanny, Galene. He smiled as he thought of the time she had left him in the nursery while she went to the kitchen for cookies and milk. When she returned, she couldn't believe what she saw. Ceilidh was having a tug of war with his dog Clancy. They were pulling on a stocking that the upstairs maid had dropped in the hall on her way to the laundry. Galene tried not to laugh as she watched the big red dog and the small boy at their game. She hoped that the Queen Mother, Victoria, could see the funny side of the story when she heard about it. The stocking matched her newest ball gown.

"Ceilidh, let go. You have torn up my good stocking." She pointed to a small chair and sternly aid, "Sit here." Clancy began to prance around. He had won the game. He took the stocking and laid down on his favorite rug by the hearth and began to chew.

The hardest part of Galene's job as nanny was when she had to discipline the young prince. In a firm voice she said, "Do you understand that you have destroyed something that does not belong to you? As your punishment, you will stay inside while Gus and I go for our daily walk.

Gus was Ceilidh's cousin that was visiting for the summer from the most northern part of Vergen from the small hamlet of Bowdoinham.

Tears rolled down Ceilidh's cheeks as he thought of all the fun things he would miss. His two favorite things were chasing squirrels and climbing the apple tree to look for bird nests.

Each year Vergen celebrated the "Festival of Bounty" the people were especially excited this year because their king planned to visit every corner of the kingdom in search of a bride.

Sir Gordon, Ceilidh's most trusted palace worker, had planned the trip. He had assigned two of his bravest warriors to act as body guards for the king. Elio and Nic considered this a great honor and pledged to do their utmost to make Sir Gordon proud of them.

Every subject waved and cheered as the king and his group rode from the palace. They would eagerly await King Ceilidh's return with the maiden who would be his bride and their Queen.

"Skinny Simmie"

Our country suffered a shock October 29, 1929 that history records as Black Tuesday. On that day we entered the Great Depression that was to grip the nation for the next decade. The stock market on Wall Street plunged to an all time low and fortunes were lost in every walk of life. People committed suicide by jumping from windows of skyscrapers unable to cope with the pressure of financial ruin. Some financial tycoons were reduced to selling pencils and apples on the streets, others stood in bread lines.

Life went on and things settled down to a daily routine of doing whatever was necessary to survive until December 26 in a sleepy little town where the Little Kanawha River flows into the Ohio a feat unheard of at that time took place. A 34-year-old white woman gave birth to a black baby girl.

This was proclaimed to the neighborhood as my brother Paul and sister Wilma ran down two flights of stairs onto Swann Street and yelled to everyone that would listen, "Mother has a nigger baby and she's ugly as sin."

We were new on the block because it was easier to move often than argue with the landlord about paying the rent. A steady stream of visitors followed in and out of the three room flat in the next couple of days. Most were disappointed when they left and made comments like, "Why Donnie, she's not black and not too ugly, just red and kinda fat for a girl."

Thus started the big adventure of the life of Betty Frances Simmons. This event was not recorded in history as was the start of the Great Depression, but it was the beginning of an exciting time for me.

My 15-year-old sister, Zada didn't care one way or the other about my arrival because she was employed as a dishwasher in a restaurant after school and wasn't home much to hear me cry and demand all the things babies seem to think they need.

Wilma and Paul slowly accepted the fact that I was there to stay after Mother told them it was impossible to send me back as they suggested. She had given birth six times and knew I was a bonafide member of the family now. Two of my older brothers died as infants.

The next period of my life was quit pleasant as I was watched over by whom ever wasn't busy while Mother cleaned housed for $3.00 a week to support us. My father ditched his family responsibilities before I was born so we were on our own. I was referred to as the cute little gal with long brown curls and allowed to do anything I took a fancy to.

This worked fine until one day this lady came to the door and inquired if Mother would like to enroll me in school. They talked and I forgot the matter completely and I went on being the baby of the family and doing exactly as I pleased until one day my world collapsed around me.

Mother announced, "Betty, today you start to school," and my response was "I'm not going to any ole school!" I was coaxed and pleaded with but I stood firm. The neighbors tried to bribe me with candy. I snatched the peppermint stick from them but I had no intention of leaving my security where I was queen.

In desperation my wise mother said okay. I'll go and you can stay here by yourself. She started slowly up the walk and when I saw she meant business I began following about a half block behind. What else was I to do? I had never been left alone and didn't know what to do, so I followed. She waited for me at the front door of the school and we went in together and met Miss Wertenbaker, the lady who helped shape my life for the next two years.

Thus my formal education started at the two room Willard School on Staunton Avenue on September 1935. My teacher had a way with spoiled kids and after a few circle games and being caught in London Bridge, Miss Wertenbaker had me hooked.

Orange drink and chocolate milk are my fondest memories of my first two years of school. I also saw thing like crayons and chalk for the first time. Somewhere in the middle of these fascinating new things I learned to read from a book about Ann and her cat.

I lived for recess and the chance to ride on the teeter-totter and swing on a horizontal metal bar on the playground. The bar was a real challenge outfitted in a dress and long brown slick cotton stockings. The idea was to see who could swing the highest without hitting your head on the ground while hanging with your legs draped around the bar without showing your underwear.

I wondered who was tall enough to have written all the neat ABC's that were posted at the top of the blackboard. I'd never been to a circus so I thought that the school hired a man on stilts. Maybe it was the job for the tall man when the circus came to town.

I learned many things and finally graduated across the hall to third grade. I've wondered in later years if I played a part in pushing my teacher over the brink because shortly after I completed second grade she was admitted to Weston State Hospital for the mentally disturbed.

Most of my health needs were met with home remedies such as mustard plasters slapped on me to loosen a tight chest, or Bone Set tea to make you sweat with the end result of it helping no matter what you complained of. I thought the taste was horrible until I was introduced to a concoction made from yellow root, which was the pits.

My playmate that lived in the upstairs apartment was sick and I was told to stay home, but my curiosity got the best of me. I couldn't understand why everyone was talking about Willa, why the doctor had been to see her, and why a man came and put an important-looking paper on her door.

One day while Mother was at work and my sister was busy scrubbing the kitchen floor, I sneaked out and went up the side steps to check things out. Willa was in bed playing with her paper dolls. She was so glad to see me because I was the first little girl that had come to play. She was forbidden to get out of bed so I set up things for a tea party and we had crackers that I had brought in my pocket from home and water. I had crept to the bathroom and brought the water back in the only cup I could find. Being told many times that I would have to learn to share, I decided to give it a try and I let Willa have every other drink, but I still had to be first.

Somehow I got in and out of that house without anyone the wiser, until two weeks later when my crime was discovered.

When Mother came from work one evening, she took a look at me and said, "Are you okay? You look red." I didn't want to confess that my head hurt and my throat felt like I didn't want any cornbread or pork rinds. I knew the routine and was told to lie quietly while she brewed the Bone Set tea.

The next day the neighbors advised Mother she had better call a doctor to check me over if she didn't want the law at her door. I don't remember her now but a nice lady doctor came and said that I indeed had scarlet fever and was to stay in bed for three weeks. She also reported the case to the Health Department and the entire family was put under quarantine.

I then knew what the sign had said on Willa's door. At this point I made a full confession and asked for mercy. The family felt sorry for me because I was sick so they didn't say much. I can only imagine what they were thinking.

Antibiotics were not a part of the treatment at that time and as a result of the high temperature over an extended period, my skin peeled. I remember the scales in the bed and Mother changing the sheets and washing them in a tub on a washboard. That tea party had upset the whole family.

I didn't really think about being deprived. I was never hungry and at the end of every month when Mother got her $40 pay from working on the W.P.A. sewing project we had beef ribs for Sunday dinner. Mother walked two miles to the sewing center in South Parkersburg and made buttonholes in shirts by hand all day.

The workers were given a lunch period and were permitted to knit if they had extra time after eating. The yarn was furnished and by eating fast Mother created a pink sweater with pink ribbon around the neck that had little pompoms hanging at the ends. It was the most beautiful thing I had ever seen. I didn't realize how special the sweater was until I learned years later that she had never knitted before and was learning as she worked.

I learned at an early age that book satchels and red pencil boxes were beyond my reach and I was sure those little girls in Brownie Scout uniforms were the chosen few. They had special dresses, beanies, and socks in additions to money for dues every week. I tried not to let my disappointment show.

I was lifted up the social ladder when I was asked to join the Sunshine Club. A neighborhood mother had turned an upstairs bedroom into a club room and we met every Tuesday evening. It was the biggest house I had ever set foot in. I remember carving a duck from a bar of Ivory Soap and playing games. The dues were two cents a week and when our leader found out that I couldn't always pay she took me aside and told me I could come anyway. I was first introduced to Kool-Aid and sugar cookies at the club. It was a great feeling to belong to a special group. Mrs. Florence was a kind and caring lady that saw a need to reach out to kids like me.

I don't know where the money for a ten-cent ticket came from but I saw movies at the Palace Theatre on 7th Street. Gene Autry and Champ, Roy Rogers and Trigger were my heroes and I was carried away in a world of make believe with the 3 Stooges and the Dead End Kids, the black and white cartoons of Mickey Mouse and Donald Duck, and the Three Little Pigs were always welcome before the movie feature. While we were walking home from the movies and if we had the money, we stopped at the Pure Dairy store and got two big dips of ice cream in a cone for a nickel. My favorite was orange pineapple.

I spent many evenings at the neighbor's house listening to Jack Armstrong the "All American Boy" on the radio. I was never to find out if the Wheaties that sponsored the program was as good as the announcer said, we ate oats every morning except when we had brown poor mans gravy and biscuits.

Birthdays were not celebrated in our family except by my older sister Zada whose birthday was December 31. She bought herself a cake, usually angel food and we put a candle on it and we watched the New Year come in.

My mother was obsessed with protecting me. I was never allowed to play with dangerous toys. My brother got in big trouble the day he strapped roller skates on my shoes. Mother caught him before I even got to stand up and told him to take them back to the kid he had borrowed them from.

Later that same day Jimmy from across the street came with his bicycle and he and Paul thought it would be great fun to take me for a ride. I was holding on to the handle bars with both hands as we whizzed up the sidewalk when my brother who was running along beside me saw Mother on the porch. He was caught red handed and was given a tongue lashing about trying to kill his little sister.

One day when Mother and the big kids had finished working in the garden, they decided to cool off by wading in nearby Worthington Creek. Everyone was having a great time until I slipped on a rock in a riffle and began screaming like a banshee. I wasn't hurt, my hair didn't even get wet, but Mother laid the law down. "You can't go in the water again until you learn to swim." To this day I can't roller skate, ride a bike, or swim.

My religious training was sporadic. Wilma started me to Sunday School at the Liberty Street Church of God and I had a teacher named Mrs. Jones that gave us little cards with bible stories on them and we had books that we pasted gold stars in for coming and red stars when we missed. She also gave me a handkerchief for my birthday.

Mother took me to a revival service that was held in a big room over a rollicking beer joint. I don't remember what kind of church it was but a man drew pictures with colored sand and preached as he drew. The lights were dimmed with the pictures spotlighted. It was the only art work I had ever seen unless you count the big lion's head on the front of my school tablet that Mother learned to copy. I don't know what the Budweiser drinkers thought when we sang "The Old Rugged Cross."

My traveling was limited to my Uncle Shell coming in his car and taking us to their house in Vienna for a visit. They moved later and we visited their family by Mother hitchhiking with me part way and riding a train the last nine miles Jo my cousin had all kinds of toys including big dolls and a cast iron stove that you could build a fire in and cook real food. They also had a player piano and a Victrola.

The food was beyond anything I had ever seen with milk, butter, cheese, and meat served at every meal. Aunt Mae did the family wash on a wringer washer with a gasoline powered motor. My uncle worked for the gas company and I thought they lived a life of luxury.

I was also taken for visits to my mother's friend's house. She had met Ida while working on the sewing project and I looked forward to seeing her. She was not only a friendly lady but she had a dog and lived on a houseboat. I dreamed of sailing down the Little Kanawha River with Rover at my side to seek my fortune and see the rest of the world.

We managed to have a Christmas tree and Santa Clause always brought me a doll and play dishes. I think Wilma and Paul were Santa's helpers with money they earned by selling newspapers on the street. I remember seeing Santa at the Kresge 5 & 10¢ store but I was too shy to talk to him. After we left I cried because I wanted a blue pocketbook with a silver chain handle and was sure that I wouldn't get it. A neighbor, Mrs. Shreves was with us and volunteered to go back to the store and tell Santa. He must have understood how important it was because on Christmas morning, that pocketbook was under the tree.

By the year 1940 Mother had put together enough furniture for adequate living. We had an icebox and a card with numbers on it that we hung in the window to tell the delivery man how much ice we wanted. We usually got 25 pounds for a dime. We had a kitchen stove with tall legs and an oven on the side. We also had a couch and a chair that didn't match.

I had started 5th grade at Jefferson School and all was going okay until I came home from school and found the house in an uproar. Almost all our furniture was gone including the heating stoves and the washer that Mother was still making payments on. The furniture had been stolen while no one was home and there was no insurance. The police couldn't help us so Mother and I started over.

We left the house with what we could carry. The older kids were on their own by this time. We stayed anyplace that people had a days work for Mother which she did for our room and board. I attended five schools that year including Jefferson, Nash, Tavernerville, and Garfield in Parkersburg where most of the time I didn't have books. Sometimes the other kids would let me look at theirs.

My last two weeks at Garfield school I had books after the teacher suggested I withdraw my money from the school savings bank account that I had built up to almost $3.00 in the past three years. We had a bank book at school and every Wednesday was deposit day. I rarely had more than 2 or 3 cents at a time, but I was proud of the fact that I had money in the bank. The account was closed and I paid rent on the books that I used for two weeks. In February of that year we moved in with Aunt Zelma and Uncle Fritz in Ritchie County and I finished the school year at a one room school named Cedar Grove. My cousin Billy was in the same grade and I could use his books. I probably would have failed 5th grade if it hadn't been for a young teacher that helped me catch up with the rest of the class.

My aunt helped by sending such neat things as biscuits and ham or jelly and homemade light bread sandwiches to school in my own four-pound lard pail. I had a tin cup to get water from the school pump in the yard. I remember when she ordered clothing for Billy from Spiegels Catalog that I always got something. One time it was a pair of socks and another I got a red silk hair ribbon with a clasp on it.

During my stay with them I was introduced to chores such as carrying water up the hill from the spring, picking black and huckleberries and churning butter. Mr. Hedges "put on a play" at school and we done so well that we were asked to present it at the big two room school at King Knob for their PTA meeting. I can't remember my part but I loved every minute of it.

We moved to the nearby Hill Farm where I was to spend the next three years. We lived first in a room over a cellar and it was great having a place of our very own once again. The farm was made up of the main two story house, a two-room house with a porch and a bigger house of four rooms with a small porch. When the youngest son moved to town we rented the two room house and lived like queens. We graduated to the four room dwelling when an older son moved to Ohio to work in a defense plant.

Life was good, my granddad lived only a mile away and I only had to walk one and a half miles to the school bus.

In the summer Mother raised a garden and I learned to can vegetable and pickle corn and beans in a 10-gallon jar. We had a cellar and our own private outside toilet.

The family in the big house had two girls so I didn't have to walk to school alone. We got on the bus at Welch's Store at Mahone and rode a mile to the King Knob School. Mr. Summers was my 6th grade teacher and Mr. Britton saw me through the 7th and 8th grade. I remember playing prisoner's base and red rover on the playground. I was taunted by some mean boys with names like "Slim" and "Skinny-Simmie." Two other girls were tall also and we towered over all the other kids.

The school presented a play with the main plot built around three old ladies and guess who got the choice parts? Lulu, Anita, and I got a standing ovation from the PTA group. Mother thought nothing of walking two and a half miles with me to school for things that were held at night like PTA meetings and pie socials.

She got a certificate for reading 12 books from the school library one year. The library consisted of some shelves with about 100 books including the reference books. Many parents had their children bring books home for them because there was nothing else available to read unless you could afford the county paper.

I read <u>Call</u> of <u>the</u> <u>Wild</u>, <u>Little</u> <u>Women</u>, and many others over the three years in that school. Reading wasn't bad at night because the house we lived in had free piped in gas with mantel lights.

Lunch at school was cooked in one of the cloak rooms and we ate at our desks. It was free for everyone. We had powdered milk and eggs and whatever else the government was passing out that month.

Mother and I used to take a feed sack and go to the country store once a month and get our commodities off the truck as it came by. They also passed out clothing at times. I was glad to get the food, but I hated it when another girl came to school with a dress like I was wearing that day. Everyone knew where they came from. Mine always fit because mother altered them. She didn't have a sewing machine but she did well by hand.

We did okay with the garden, the things from the truck and the $12 dollars a month that mother got to support me with from the state.

Before I started 7th grade, Wilma came to visit and brought me a see-through plastic raincoat, a book satchel with a shoulder strap, a lunch pail with a tray in top of it and a pencil box. Zada bought me a snowsuit like some of the other kids had. I thought I was set for life.

The county sent a music teacher around every two weeks and she taught us the patriotic songs that were popular during the war. I first heard about Pearl Harbor on a little radio that was on a table in front of our class room. Penmanship was emphasized in school and there were days when we spent a whole hour making ovals and push and pulls. I don't know what it did for my writing but you sure learned to stick with a task.

I was a lieutenant in the school patrol sponsored by AAA. I wore a white canvas belt that fit over one shoulder and around the waist. It had a blue metal badge pinned to the canvas. Each day before lunch I was privileged to carry one of the wooden man sized forms to the middle of the road that ran by the school and place it in a hole in the pavement. A picture of a state policeman was painted on the form and a catchy little verse reminded the drivers to slow down in the school area. After the last recess I brought it back to the school building The school patrolmen were treated to a trip to Washington at the end of the school year but the trips were canceled during the war years.

We continued to see Aunt Zelma and Uncle Fritz and we walked the three miles to the Indian Creek United Brethenn Church. Later they moved to Preston County where my uncle went to work in the coal mines.

During the three years that we lived in Ritchie County I saw my Granddad Reed often and looked on him as a father figure. He was a strong Republican and liked to tease me by calling me Democrat. My Grandma Clara died when I was five years old and later granddad married Alice. She was a kind lady and we got along great. She had not had the opportunity to go to school and I taught her to write her name. She liked to call me Francie.

I enjoyed history and missed taking the Golden Horseshoe test by two points. (In later years I was given the privilege of seeing our four daughters awarded Golden Horseshoes in impressive ceremonies at the state Capitol.) I finished eighth grade in May 1943 and we moved to Wood County and lived with Zada in an apartment under a restaurant.

Coming straight from the country, I thought it was a noisy place. I was used to peace and quiet except when the whippoorwill called in the evening or the cows bawled when the farmer was late with his milking chores. We lived there a few months and then moved to near by Hogland Run to a three-room house.

I started to Parkersburg High School in September where the enrollment was near 3,000 students. The 27-acre campus served grades seven through twelve. Homemaking was my favorite subject because of Marion Layton a teacher that I respected and tried hard to please. She made home visits to check our projects that we were required to work on at home.

Before I entered 10th grade we moved across the road to what was referred to as the big house on the Hively Farm. It had six rooms, a pitcher pump in the kitchen and electricity. There was also space for a yard and a garden. I didn't move again until September 1947 when I went to the hospital to study nursing.

The family was supportive in my school work but since I was farther along than any of them had gone in school, when I needed help in math our neighbor Mr. Miracle came to my rescue.

They helped by asking questions before a test and gathering leaves and wild flowers for biology class. Mother even went to parents night at school and went through my classes including working the combination of my locker. That was a great accomplishment for someone who had only finished the 5th grade before she was kept home from school to help care for younger brothers and sisters. She had survival skills that can only be learned by meeting difficult situations with determination and hard work.

My home-economics. class was divided by cooking one semester and sewing the next. We were divided into groups of five for cooking where we prepared a dish and were required to eat it to make a passing grade. I still wonder today if I would have been better off to have taken the F for the day than to have eaten a bean casserole that we made. Apparently we doubled some of the ingredients and left others out. The taste was beyond description but we made a pact not to let Miss Layton know. When she came to check on our progress, we were all sitting around the table smiling and trying not to gag. Cooking was the easier of the two groups for me.

What I knew about sewing could be fitted into a thimble. My experience was limited to watching mother sew on a button and patch something by hand. I almost wore out an 8x10 inch piece of cloth learning the different stitches, making button holes and sewing on snaps.

The assignment my sophomore year was to make a dress and wear it to school. I put a side zipper in a dress seven times before it met the teacher's approval. I wore a cardigan type sweater to hide the zipper on the day I had to wear the dress to school. I thought I had covered up my disgrace until I entered the home-economics class room and was told immediately to take my sweater off and model for the class.

The other girls didn't laugh because some of them also had limited skills, while others started the year knowing many fine points of the sewing machine. I don't know what happened, whether it was Mrs. Layton's patience or my stubborn streak that made me say, if they can do it so can I.

The next year I made an outfit of a wool pleaded skirt with a zipper, a lined weskit, and a long sleeve blouse with French cuffs. I was one of the few chosen to model the outfit in a style show at the professional women's club.

The office workers who handled scheduling of classes made a mistake and put me in an advanced algebra class without any previous knowledge of algebra or geometry. The teacher caught on that I was hopelessly lost after the first quiz and decided that I should be scheduled for something else. I stayed on in that class until a decision was made by the office to put me in a geometry class. I don't think much thought was given to the move, it was probably the only place there was a vacant chair. Remember they were trying to educate 3,000 kids. I was a month behind the class and with no one to help me at home, I was in a complete daze from day one.

The teacher vented her anger by yelling at me for signing up for geometry before taking beginning algebra. Some kind soul rescued me and shipped me to a business math class where I worked my way around percentages and decimals with flying colors.

I struggled with junior English and spent all my free time in the class room with other kids who weren't quite sure what an adverb modified. We also were supposed to be memorizing passages from Edgar Allen Poe's works and probably other authors that I have long since forgotten. The parts of speech just seemed to fall in place after I was exposed to Latin the following year.

I lived for Mr. Spencer's chemistry class. I liked to see all the chemicals fizz in the test tubes and I liked the math and pondering over the equations. My grades of A's in that class helped lift my spirits when I thought of my struggles with Shakespeare and Julius Caesar.

I graduated with a class of 622 and I hadn't met some of the kids in my class until we were lined up for com-mencement practice. I was in front of Betty Jane Simmons and behind Mary Sue Simmons.

My first paying job was at a restaurant on Emerson Avenue where I washed dishes, mopped floors and did anything else that an inexperienced 14-year-old was capable of. I was only there a few months until I heard of this fantastic sounding position in the dietary department at St. Joseph's Hospital.

I applied and was hired, how could they turn me down with an employment record like mine? I had visions of healing the sick by providing meals that were served on attractive trays. I had had Home-Economics in school, hadn't I? The dietitian didn't share my dream and I was assigned to Annie in the scullery where all the vegetables and fruit were prepared for the cooks. In the few months I worked there I saw brussel sprouts, asparagus, and avocados for the first time. When we caught up dicing and peeling I was sent to the dishwashing room where I scrapped food from patients' trays and stacked the dishes for the dishwasher.

From the time I started ninth grade I worked in the school cafeteria at noon for a free lunch. I got out of class early so I could eat before I started to wash silverware. Two other girls and I did nothing for an hour except wash forks and spoons. I was next put on the cafeteria line where I added the cost of the meals and wrote it on a square of paper that the student passed to the cashier at the end of the line. Each food was a different price and the calculating was done without the aid of an adding machine. I also performed similar duties in the teachers cafeteria where the prices were different. I graduated to cashier after one semester as a checker and worked there until I graduated.

I left the hospital kitchen when I got a job at the Chancellor Hotel as cafeteria cashier after school and week-ends. Mrs. Steel, my supervisor at school, and Mrs. Ashton the pastry cook, gave me a favorable recommendation for the after school job. I have gone through life believing that nothing could compare to Mrs. Ashton's pies especially the butterscotch meringue.

I started at twenty-eight cents an hour at the Chancellor. I added the price of the different foods on the cash register and collected the money. That was easier than the method I used at school When I wasn't working as cashier, I did odd jobs like "eyeing potatoes" and "backing shrimp." The potatoes were rolled into a cellar room without windows. They had been bumped and cleaned in a machine then placed in big wash tubs. My job was to remove the eyes for the cooks. When I see shrimp on a menu today I regress back to my teen age years where I see a 10-gallon pot of shrimp in the same room with the potatoes and I hear someone saying "Shell and back those as quickly as you can, you know they need to cool before Carrie can make the shrimp cocktails.

The cafeteria was decorated with tall urns of pine branches that I changed every month. The most undesirable job that I was given was the responsibility of scrapping chewing gum from the bottom of chairs and tables the same day I changed the pine. I never could understand why anyone that had enough money to eat in a nice restaurant like the Chancellor could be that crude.

I earned enough money to buy my school pictures and class ring. I also bought books and most of my clothing. The job I did in high school that I wasn't paid for but enjoyed was working in the infirmary. It was great fun watching the nurse swab throats and bandage cuts.

I hope I haven't painted a picture of all work and no play. I was a part of a trio that sang at church and had friends that I visited in the neighborhood. I had my sights set for a certain boy that came to church occasionally. Finally April 5, 1945 he noticed me and asked to walk home with me. He was worth the wait because I still have him by my side today.

The next five years were filled with movies and root beer floats when we had time away from our jobs. We decided December 24, 1949 that we knew each other well enough to get married the following August and I got an engagement ring.

In August 1947 a whole new world opened for me when I entered the St. Joseph's Hospital School of Nursing. I was to devote three years of my life to acquiring skills for caring for the sick and many things about human nature that weren't profiled in the recruiting literature.

We spent at least 12 hours every day at the hospital including classes and floor work. The students were housed in three private houses four blocks down the street with a house mother in charge. I lived first with Miss English who was a sophisticated lady that wore white gloves to meals.

The hospital had three dining rooms, the first was for nurses, the second for doctors, and the priests ate alone in the third. The nuns ate in their private living quarters on a section of the third floor of the hospital. I had never used a cloth napkin nor had I seen a napkin ring holder.

We were required to practice procedures on each other before we were allowed to try on a real patient. I did everything from giving a bed bath to learning the fine points of injections without doing my roommate Roberta any permanent harm. I must admit that it was hard to lie quietly while I was the patient. I shut my eyes and tried to pretend that Roberta knew what she was doing and that her hands weren't really shaking as she came at me with a syringe filled with normal saline solution.

The procedure class went well until time came to insert a tube down each other's noses and pump out the contents of our stomachs. The assignment to read the chapter was given on Monday with the demonstrations to be done in class on Friday. By Wednesday, half of the class had called home to ask if they could quit nursing. This was the most revolting thing that most of us had ever heard of. I didn't call. I reasoned that maybe it wouldn't be much worse than scrapping chewing gum from the bottom of tables. Besides we didn't have a phone.

Word must have filtered to administration that they were about to loose most of their first year students and the instructor was called to the office. I don't know what was said but when we went to class Miss Garrity told us we were getting behind schedule and didn't have time for everyone to demonstrate inserting a naso-gastric tube. She then said that if two people would volunteer to demonstrate the procedure they would get an A grade for the entire unit and not be required to take a written test. Everyone else would take the test in addition to writing a composition about the digestive system. We had until the next day to decide. That was the thing we all talked about that evening.

Two girls made the mistake of saying that maybe it wouldn't be too bad and less risky than making a failing grade on a test. We began to make offers and bribes to them and they decided to do it after they had in writing promises to have their beds made for a week, their laundry done and their food paid for the next time we had bedtime snacks delivered.

I watched next day as two people stood in front of our class and performed an act of bravery that saved the rest of us cowards. I passed the test and earned a B on the composition. I don't think the instructor knew of our scheme and I certainly wasn't going to say anything. I took my turn of washing clothes in the sink on a washboard and kept my mouth shut.

Our class was finally sent to the wards to meet real people. I was assigned to room 204 to do p.m. care, which consisted of cleaning people up before the supper trays came. I walked into the middle of the room and froze. In my wildest dream I couldn't imagine anyone expecting me to care for a man before I had practiced on little old ladies. My expression was a dead give away, there was not one man but one in each corner bed of the room and in that moment I forgot everything I had learned in class.

The older of the four men took pity on me and said, "We usually start by getting a pan of water." One of the younger guys snickered but quieted down when the first man told him to "give the girlie a chance." My hero walked me through the job step by step and when the supervisor came to check my ward she took points off my grade for not hanging the towel correctly on the rack. I carried a soft spot in my heart for that group of men that helped me over my first hurdle.

At the end of six months we were "capped" in an impressive ceremony in the hospital chapel. I spent most of my first year on second floor trying to meet the high standards of the nurse who was in charge of the women's wing and her colleague who was the supervisor for the men's wards.

Their domineering personalities must have helped shape my attitude toward nursing in later life but it was hard for an 18-year-old to see why it was important to be called out of bed after working the night shift, to dress and walk four blocks back to the hospital to remove a magazine from a window sill. The complaint "You left the room messy."

Each student took a turn working in the diet kitchen where we were responsible for fixing all the special diets. We made out the menus, cooked the food, delivered trays to the patients and cleaned the diet kitchen. We washed the pots and pans and utensils that we used by hand. When the special trays were brought back to the dishwashing room we checked to see what had not been eaten. The food that was left on a diabetic tray was measured and weighed and we converted the calories to orange juice. We delivered this to the charge nurse for the patient, to be used if needed to balance their insulin medicine until the next meal.

We were then free to go home or to class if one was scheduled for that evening. The hours were usually 7a.m. to 7p.m. with time off in the afternoon to go to class.

We were supposed to get one day off each week which was usually the day we had most classes. Somehow the scheduling got fouled up and I spent seven weeks in the kitchen without a day off. I never again wanted to hear the dietitian say "Are your menus ready for me to check," or "have you calculated the calories needed for the diabetics that didn't eat well?"

You might say that I jumped out of the frying pan into the fire when I was told to report to the OB Department. I had never touched a kid under two years of age and knew nothing about the birthing process except what I'd read in a book. We started by caring for the new mothers then graduated to the nursery. That was fun after I discovered that the babies wouldn't break when I touched them.

The real challenge came when I was sent to the labor and delivery area. I was under the watchful eye of an experienced RN that knew the ropes. I finally was told to scrub for my 1st delivery and help the doctor. He was an egotistical grouch who didn't want a student near him. He thought he deserved only RN's to assist him. He eyed me over and said, "Who sent you in here?" I was too scared to answer so he just put up with me. It was lucky that he wasn't the only doctor that brought new life into the world because each student had to have 25 scrubs to pass the course.

During the three months I spent on OB I was on call and slept on a cot in a room on third floor. I worked a couple of weeks on the medical floor before I was assigned to surgery.

I don't remember what I thought the work in the operating room would be like, maybe I'd just stand in the background for a while and watch the mighty surgeons at work. I was jolted back to the real world when I reported to the nun in charge the first day. She whisked me off down the hall to the doctors' dressing room and told me to clean the scum off the shower walls and then to scour the sinks with Bon Ami.

I must have done a good job because the next day I was promoted to polishing the doctors' white shoes which included washing the shoe strings. I progressed on to washing bloody sponges on a washboard, then washing mops and taking them to the roof top to dry. Next I washed gloves and put them on a rack to dry.

I had begun to think I was never to see the inside of an operating room when one afternoon after a busy schedule I was permitted to go in a room and help wash blood off the walls. I was making my mark because when it became evident that I could follow orders and not faint at the sight of blood, I was allowed to gown up and actually watch somebody loose their gallbladder.

Each student had to scrub for 25 major and 50 minor cases to meet the requirements set up by the nursing department. I again slept on the narrow cot on third floor for what seemed like an eternity while I counted the scrubs each day.

The nun on the pediatric floor was a deeply spiritual lady that told us everyday she expected only the best from us because God had entrusted his children to our care. I acquired many skills while working on pediatrics but what I remember most is the ability of Sister De Lourdes to show love and compassion for the parents and children that she came in contact with daily.

The hospital had an agreement with St. Francis Hospital in Pittsburgh for all of the students to do a three month rotation in their facility for the mentally ill. We were sent in groups of five and I was amazed at all the new things I saw from the time I stepped off the bus in the biggest city I had ever been in. In the next three months I saw shock treatments given, learned the buddy system for making night bed checks, carved a key chain, embroidered a scarf and danced the polka with the patients.

The food in the dining room was good and I remember barley soup and homemade bread being served every meal including breakfast.

When we returned to Parkersburg I started marking off the days on the calendar until I would graduate and be free. I wrote the last will and testament for our class and couldn't help but remember some of the fun things like a spook house at a Halloween party. I also remember the party that was given by the sisters of De Sales Heights where we all wore fancy long dresses. We went to the academy for a chemistry class taught by Sister Consolota. It was one of the most enjoyable classes in my three years of study.

We had a graduation exercise at St. Xavier Church in May and we wore long sleeve white uniforms and were permitted to wear a black band on our cap. We were given unsigned diplomas and sent back to the hospital to complete our time. Sister Virginia signed my diploma at 10:00 a..m. August 5,1950 and at 6:30 p.m. the same day I started a new phase of my life by marring the guy I had met five years earlier. The Reverend Ofa Bennett of Dickerson Avenue in

Vienna performed the ceremony in his home with his wife and daughter acting as witnesses.

Our first home was a three room furnished apartment at 412 Eleventh Street. Between us we had a 16 piece set of dishes, a pair of pillow cases which were gifts from our families and a wooden box with tools in it. We shared a bathroom with Mrs. Parker our landlady and took our clothes to the laundromat. Our family routine was upset when I had an emergency appendectomy in November.

I had taken the state board test for RN licensure in October and the results came a week before Christmas. I celebrated by hanging the paper on top of the Christmas tree with a red ribbon.

Our first separation came when Vic was drafted into the army in Feb, 1951 during the Korean War. I continued to work at the hospital and soon after he left I moved to 502 Hickory Street and acquired a few pieces of furniture.

By then we knew that in August we would need a baby bed and I began to save pennies in a jar toward the purchase of one. What was to become the family crib was bought at Dils Department Store and is in good condition today with the third mattress still usable. Vic was home to greet Jean when she arrived at 2:30 a.m. August 27, 1951. He almost had to leave before she was born because his furlough was about up. He left when she was 3 days old and was to see her next when she was three months old as he was coming from Ft. Lewis, Wash. to the east coast on his way to Germany for 14 months.

This motherhood thing was all new to me. Jean would have been better off with a bachelor or a plumber taking care of her. Everything I knew about babies I had learned in a controlled hospital setting. I had no younger brothers or sisters and had never baby-sat for anyone.

She weighed 7 lbs. ½ ounce at birth and 6 lbs. at six weeks old. She cried and I didn't know why. I made trips to the doctors' offices, the last one being to a well-known pediatrician. I was given medicine and advice but nothing seemed to work, she continued to cry.

By this stage of the game I was crying along with her a lot of the time. It didn't help much to be told "It's only the colic and she'll outgrow it." I was about to the end of my rope when a family friend that had raised ten kids suggested "all she needs is a little catnip tea and some Carnation Milk with a dab of dark Karo syrup in it." I followed her advice and a miracle took place. Jean ceased to cry and her belly button finally healed.

Nothing was too good for our first born so I extended my credit and bought an automatic washer to wash her diapers in. I was getting her clothes clean by washing them by hand but the blankets were hard to wring.

My mother came to live with me and I moved to a garage apartment on 19th street that was closer to my work at the hospital. I had never learned to drive but I decided now was the time because I needed transportation.

I checked the classified ads in the paper and found a 1941 Plymouth that sounded like my cup of tea. I called the number and went to see the car. The owner and I agreed on a price and I bought it with the stipulation that he drive it home for me. I now had a car parked at my door that I didn't have a clue how to drive.

My sister Zada came to my rescue and spent many nerve-wracking hours with me at the wheel. My brother-in-law Harold, who was a professional truck driver helped also.

I'm sure hauling freight on the highways was an easier job than riding with me.

The first time I went to take the driver's test I sailed through the written part but couldn't get the car started. The officer looked at me and said "I think you need to practice a little more." My sister didn't loose her cool, but patiently helped me log some more practice time. I passed the second time. This didn't qualify me for the Indy 500 but I was able to get around town by using the back streets.

Nursing has many sides as I was to find out while doing private duty. I spent seven weeks with a lady who was recovering from a broken hip. She had three nurses and my main job on the third shift was to put curlers in her hair every evening. The money was good and the experience was invaluable. I didn't know at that time I would become the private beautician to four famous red headed ladies.

I continued to watch my daughter grow as I waited for her father to return from Germany. I had some tense moments like the time she tumbled down the stairs and landed on a concrete floor. She had a toy telephone in her hand and it rang as it hit the steps on the way down. I went to the hardware store and bought a baby gate as soon as she stopped crying and I found she was okay except for a bump on her head.

She was the darling of the neighborhood with curly red hair. Who could resist her request when she stood at the neighbor's gate and begged for cookies.

When Jean was seventeen months old Vic came home and they got acquainted. She was not used to being around men but soon learned that having a "daddy" could be great fun. During the summer of 1952 my sister Zada took me, my mother, Jean and a friend on a car trip to the

Midwest. We visited in Colorado and took a tourist side trip to Pikes Peak.

Vic had started to work for the Power Company as a temporary employee in January 1950, and when he returned from the army he was given a permanent job. In 1953 he was transferred to Elizabeth to work as a district representative.

The next two years were pleasant as we tried to blend into life in a small town. I joined the Woman's Club and the Baptist Church. Jean attended Bible School and not only did she bring home the crafty things kindergarten children make, but the whooping cough as well. A family sent their kids to church and promptly shared their bug with the entire church. Jean had had the shot to prevent whooping cough but the antibodies had not had time to build up.

I guess the biggest event while I lived in Elizabeth was the arrival of our second daughter Vicki on February 13,1954. Life was never to be the same again. She came with the determination to break her sister's record in the length of time she could cry as a newborn.

I had no way nor the inclination to keep records, but she did well. We slept at twenty minute intervals around the clock when we weren't giving Jean enough care so the authorities wouldn't arrest us for child neglect.

I was at least smart enough to not try to breast feed her. She was given Carnation milk from day one and gained weight like a regular kid. The baby carriage that we had borrowed from her Aunt Geneva needed new tires when we returned it. We spent many hours with her in the carriage while we pushed it back and forth with our foot while lying on the bed. She was also happy propped up on your knees while you sat up in bed and kept your knees moving. We learned to keep the momentum going and doze for a minute before she realized that I wasn't moving fast enough to suit her.

Vicki's first check up at the doctor revealed an infected finger from banging it on the sides of the carriage as she cried if I failed to keep the wheels turning. She also had an infected eye. The screaming quieted down after two months and things were better until Jean decided to take care of her little sister.

She went in the bedroom with Vicki and locked the door. No amount of coaxing or threatening could get her to open the door. Her father came from work and tore a window screen off and rescued the two. Vicki was none the worse for that little episode and I never did know what Jean did in those two hours.

Vicki learned to sit up and walk at an early age. She liked to explore and I decided that Christmas would be less stressful if I didn't have to keep telling Vicki to leave the tree alone. I tied the floor pieces of the playpen to the sides and set the Christmas tree in the middle. I decorated it and stood back and admired the great job that I had done, thinking how clever I'd been by putting it in the playpen.

I was in the kitchen when I heard a strange noise that sent me running to the living room. There was Vicki looking pleased with herself. She had moved playpen and tree to the other side of the room, scattering ornaments and tinsel as she went. I had failed to remove the wheels from the legs of the playpen. That was one of many lessons I was to learn about trying to out wit her. It wasn't an easy task.

Vicki's interest in birds began when she would take all the bread she could find in the house and tear it into pieces and scatter it in the back yard. She had great fun watching the birds come to feed until I discovered the family's bread for the next couple of days was gone.

I also learned that all the food had to be removed from the table immediately after eating. If you turned your back, she would empty everything that was left into one serving dish. A mixture of spinach, mashed potatoes and milk was quite a mess.

I didn't know what one of the neighbors meant when she said "Your baby is an active little girl isn't she?" I later found out that she was passing the house and saw Vicki stretched up against the window glass hanging onto the frame like a monkey.

We placed a five-foot fence around the back yard to keep her at home. It didn't work, she could climb any place she could get a toe hold. In place of a baby gate like most parents used we nailed a piece of plywood across the end of the porch with the slick side in. This slowed her down to a degree. Jean was given the job of telling us if she saw Vicki walking a narrow porch rail that was five feet from the ground. She never fell but I lost count of the times I lifted her from the railing.

She could scale to the top bunk bed without the use of a ladder. I learned to live with that until the day she pushed a chest over and blocked the entrance to the bedroom. She sat on the top bunk and watched with interest as I tried to move the drawers and retrieve their contents that were scattered all over the floor.

Vicki was introduced to a cup when I caught her running through the house with the nipple of a glass bottle clinched in her teeth and swinging it from side to side. I might add that she could sit on top of the refrigerator so opening the door and getting a bottle was no problem. She hadn't mastered turning the nipple up so the bottles were safe if the nipple was turned down and the cap screwed on tightly.

That night I took all the bottles and hid them in the garage and her bottle days were over.

Vicki didn't seem to miss the bottles as she was too busy planning her next adventure. One day we were visiting at a neighbor's house down the street, and before we knew what was happening, Vicki had gotten the Joy liquid dish washing soap from under the sink and was joyfully skating around the kitchen floor in bubbles above her knees.

Another time, a friend was watching Vicki one day while I went to the grocery store. When I came back from shopping, a crowd had gathered in the backyard and Vicki was the center of attention. School bus drivers and other school personnel were chipping away at a tile drain that she had her foot caught in. I was too embarrassed to ask anyone to watch her after that. Elizabeth was a small town and soon everyone knew about the Ingram kid and the drain pipe.

When she was disciplined or told not to do something, she would stop immediately. But while I was cleaning up the mess, she would go on to something new. We had to keep the bathroom door locked because Vicki liked to turn the gas off in the hot water tank. Every time Jean wanted in the bathroom the door had to be unlocked.

I wondered if Vicki would make it to her 2nd birthday and if I would be sane if she did. One day I heard screams and what sounded like breaking glass. When I went to check I found that Vicki had overturned a small rocking chair and ran her head through the glass of a bookcase door. The doctor could find no damage after the blood was cleaned up. He said she must have shut her eyes when she hit. When we returned from having her checked, we cleaned up the glass and turned the bookcase around facing the wall. It remained in that position for the next 10 years.

Then one day our lives changed. God dropped an angel from heaven. A 13-year-old girl who lived close by became my helper for an hour or two every day. Both girls liked her and Vicki began to learn that maybe there was more to life than exhausting her mother.

I worked the night shift in a nearby 8-bed clinic when Vic was free to be home with the girls. It was different than anything I'd done before and I enjoyed it.

We had a party for Jean on her third birthday with kids from the neighborhood invited. She had a cake baked by a woman in the town who baked cakes as a hobby. Jean got an assortment of gifts, but I remember a green chalk board as the thing she liked best. We didn't realize it at the time but that party started a tradition of having birthday parties every other year that kids were invited to. The odd year was a family celebration.

The town doctor's wife organized an Easter parade one year. Many of the kids dressed in their Easter outfits and carried baskets. They marched around town lead by Peter Cottontail.

We were given a pressure cooker by the Elizabeth Baptist Church at a farewell party on March 30, 1956 after Vic had been transferred by the Power Company to Pennsboro.

Jean started first grade in Pennsboro. I worried because her classroom was at the top of a steep flight of steps. She managed fine but I couldn't help being concerned about my first born being placed in such a dangerous situation.

Our third daughter was born on July 20, 1957 at St. Joseph's Hospital in Parkersburg. Gayle arrived 15 days late and I've often thought that she didn't come when expected because she had decided to stay put until she had her plans

71

completed on how she could continue the family tradition of crying and not sleeping for at least two months.

Her first check up at the doctor revealed a clogged tear duct and a rupture at the navel. I had thought that if I had everything in order before she was born she would sleep and eat like I'd heard that babies did. The house was spotless, the cabinets and drawers were cleaned and all the floors had two coats of wax. It didn't help.

The doctor kept changing her formula and finally on the seventh switch we ended up giving her whole milk with barley malt syrup in it. The combination seemed to agree with her but it was dirty looking in the bottles and I got many strange looks from people who probably wondered what I was giving the poor child.

She had a bottle every three hours around the clock for the first five months of her life and solid food three times a day.

There was little done besides feed her. The rest of the family ate whatever we had. Jean got proficient in fixing bologna sandwiches and cornflakes. When Vic cooked it was breakfast foods and one evening Vicki asked if breakfast was about ready.

The neighbors brought food in occasionally which we appreciated, but their biggest contribution was when they would take Gayle and her sisters to their house for a couple of hours. One of our neighbors who owned a grocery store, would put Gayle in a car bed and drive her around in the station wagon while she delivered groceries.

After about two months, Gayle didn't cry as much and the family learned to adjust to a baby who ate every three hours around the clock.

Jean had started first grade and seemed to bring home every cold and flu bug that was going around. Gayle was in St. Joseph's Hospital for 12 days when she was seven months old for pneumonia.

Jean and Vicki had recently had their tonsils out in January. That was before the time when parents were permitted to stay with children in the hospital. When we left at the end of visiting hours the evening before surgery was scheduled, Jean cried and was inconsolable until Vicki promised to take care of her sister.

We brought them home on the second day after surgery and Vicki was ready to eat anything. It was a different story with Jean. She was nauseated and was unable to retain even water. The drug store at Pennsboro was out of the medicine the doctor prescribed and we went to West Union for the suppository that finally helped.

Before the doctor decided the girls would be better off without their tonsils, we went through a period of dealing with frequent colds and bouts of croup. Vic and I probably hold the world's record of how fast a croup tent can be assembled and a dose of Ipecac syrup could be given to a croupy kid.

After the tonsillectomies the colds and the sore throats were less frequent and Gayle must have had enough antibiotics in her system from the pneumonia treatment to ward off germs because she was better also.

Our philosophy for running a household was the Family Plan. "If you live here and are a part of the family, you worked." The children were given jobs appropriate for their age and the work list posted on the refrigerator became a part of their formative years.

They like to sing while washing dishes and one day when Jean wanted to speed up the tempo, she told Vicki to stick her finger in a light bulb socket that was mounted above the sink. Vicki was standing on a wooden box and had to stretch to unscrew the bulb. She was disappointed when she put her finger in the socket and got a shock and failed to light up like a bulb as her older sister had promised.

We occasionally had a baby-sitter at Pennsboro, but most of the time the mothers in the neighborhood watched each other's children. I traded off with several other mothers. Jean could be depended on to make sure a baby-sitter followed the instructions that I had given. I never called a girl to babysit again after Jean reported that she had fed Gayle cold baby food while we were gone.

One of Vicki's regular playmates thought it was great fun to bite her. The youngster's parents tried to put a stop to it by dealing out a variety of punishments, but they didn't work. The game came to a screeching halt when I told Vicki to bite her back.

We tried to teach the girls respect for other people's property. One day Vicki brought me some spring flowers that she had gathered from our neighbor's yard. I didn't consider Vicki a hardened criminal, but I sent her to knock on the door with the bouquet in hand to confess what had happened. The neighbor felt sorry for Vicki and we remained friends until we moved to St. Marys at the end of Jean's first year of school.

Vic started as a lineman with the Power Company in St. Marys and we began adjusting to a new community. Jean and Vicki started using the public library and especially liked story time. Gayle went along in the stroller but was too young to check out books. They went to a community sponsored Bible School that was held in the school building and to the Methodist Church for Sunday School.

They started swimming lessons in the baby section at the city pool and learned the breathe-bubble technique. Jean joined the Brownies. We didn't realize that the first troop meeting Jean attended was the beginning of the family's involvement in scouting for the next 18 years.

Selling Girl Scout cookies became a yearly event and I'll always remember the first time Jean was sent home with her card to take orders. She was shy and Vicki went along to ring doorbells and offer moral support.

All three girls had chicken pox followed by impetigo. Anyone that has been the caregiver for victims of impetigo will understand when I describe my daily routine. Everyone got at least two clean changes of clothing daily and the bed linens were also washed. I was getting the procedure down pretty well until I had to deal with complications. Vicki wore her father's hard hat and shared her impetigo with him. I don't know how I avoided the malady. Maybe our guardian angel knew that someone was needed to clean and scrub for the rest of the family.

One day the girls were playing in the back yard when a German Shepherd dog bit Vicki on the face. We took her to see a doctor and called the authorities after the owners failed to produce the dog's rabies shot record. The dog was confined for 14 days and Vicki healed. That encounter didn't seem to affect Vicki's ability to draw any stray cat or dog that was wandering about the neighborhood to our house.

The entire family was served liver one time a week in an effort to raise Vicki's iron levels. I was the only one that liked the taste of liver and I tried to disguise the taste of it for the others. I fried, baked, and made a spread for sandwiches, but it did little to change the taste.

Vicki was fair skinned with light red hair and when she was seen by a new doctor and they examined her, the questioning began. I was indirectly accused of not caring for her properly and feeding her a diet of potato chips and Hershey Kisses. I knew better and would go home and continue her iron medicine and the ritual of weekly liver dishes for the family besides cooking three square meals a day. I accepted the fact that she had sensitive skin when the problems continued even after her iron levels increased.

We watched TV. while Gayle and Vicki rode stick horses with Miss Marilyn on Romper Room. I won a three-piece Revere Ware cooking set by calling in an answer to a question on a quiz program from a Wheeling TV station. Winning the first quiz qualified me to go to Wheeling and compete in a game of unscrambling names of the new season TV programs. I brought home a 21" RCA TV set because I got the most correct in the least amount of time. I remember Bonanza being one of the answers. We had bought our first TV set at Pennsboro, so we sold this one to my sister and brother-in-law.

A lot of truck gardening was done along the Ohio River and vegetable were cheap if you picked you own in the field. One day after work Vic took the back seat out of our '49 Ford and went to the corn patch. When he came back the car and trunk were loaded with corn with barely enough room left for him to drive. The canning went on all night and the last load taken off the stove about noon the next day. We paid ten cents a dozen for the corn and ended up with one hundred pints. I was too tired to move but the girls had slept all night and were raring' to go. I got through the day but was running in low gear.

We adopted a dog named Sandy at Pennsboro that someone left at our house. We gave him to our landlady to take to Bruceton Mills because he growled at Vicki while he was eating. I don't know if she was petting him or trying to spoon feed him, but Sandy didn't like it.

We hadn't lived in St. Marys long before the girls became attached to Mrs. Baily's cat. When Mittens died she had a royal funeral and was buried in the backyard.

I turned down a chance to work at the Colin Anderson Home for children that had been born with mental and physical handicaps. With three girls to care for it was a challenge to keep up with things at home.

Grandma Simmons, Aunt Wilma and Uncle Harold came early on Christmas morning to watch the girls open presents. The girls were supposed to stay upstairs until Grandma came and so it became a tradition to take the toaster and butter upstairs Christmas Eve so they could eat while they waited. It was necessary to initiate this rule after Jean and Vicki got up early one Christmas morning and were quietly playing with all their toys when we woke up. Jean could read and had sorted all the packages that were tagged for her or Vicki.

The Power Company decided that the Ingram Family had been in one place long enough and sent Vic to work in Spencer January, 1960. The rest of the family moved in May after Jean finished third grade. During those four months Vic stayed at the Spencer-Roane Hotel and ate most of his meals at family restaurant across the street. He came home on weekends when he wasn't on call.

We moved to a house on Capehart Street and the girls found a substitute grandma, a kind and caring neighbor named Mrs. Sheppard. She supported herself by sewing for people and for Gayle's third birthday she made her a blue pinafore with lace trimming.

The Power Company sponsored a picnic for employees and their families each summer. We were new to the community and looked forward to getting acquainted with other Power Company families. The picnic was held at the Roane County 4-H Camp. We were welcomed by many friendly people, the food was good, and everything was going great until I heard crying. Jean had fallen off the monkey bars in the play area and hit her left arm.

We didn't have a family doctor so we took her to Gordon's Hospital. She was admitted after the doctor had set the bone and applied a cast. His next task was to assure two nervous parents that their daughter would be as good as new in a short while.

The first day at Spencer Grade School was an experience for the entire family. I paid Vicki's first grade fees and got her settled with Miss Stemple. The next stop was Mrs. Hildreth's fourth grade room where I was given a book and supply list after I explained about the cast on Jean's arm. Gayle and I followed the crowd downtown to Murphy's store and got in line to buy books for Jean.

In the schools she had attended before, the books had been rented. I was to find out the following year that many parents sold and traded books at the beginning of school. I felt like a street hawker with a stack of books in my arms roaming the school halls calling out, "I'll trade you and English for a math book."

Word got around that Jean's books were a bargain because she took good care of them. We couldn't save them for Vicki because they would probably change in three years. We moved up the street to another house on Capehart in

September 1960. We rented until 1973 when we bought the house, which was know as the old Ryan property. We made improvements to the house throughout the years as money became available.

On October 19, Vic and I got up at 5a.m. and decided to take an early morning walk around the neighborhood. We stopped to chat with Helen and her sister Hazel at Gordon's Hospital and with the help of the doctor, we welcomed daughter #4 at 7:30 a.m. to the family. I was resigned to a repeat performance of crying and staying awake for weeks when I took Kelli home from the hospital. The doctor had supplied me with a bottle of drops to use if she had symptoms of colic, but they were never used. I had heard stories about babies that slept all night but I didn't believe any of them.

A few days after Kelli came home I put her in the crib at 9 p.m. and went to bed soon after. I woke later and glanced at the clock,. Fear gripped me as I saw it was 2 a.m. I was sure Kelli had suffocated in her sleep and that I had been a bad mother because I hadn't heard her when she cried out for help. Unable to hold back the tears, I crept into her room. There she lay sleeping peacefully and content with the world. All of a sudden I was struck with the realization that the tales I heard about babies that cried only when they were hungry or wet could be true.

I became actively involved in scouting as troop leader, day camp worker, and spent time at Camp Sandy Bend. I was a camp consultant and taught outdoor skills at troop meetings. The scouts earned badges by meeting requirements related to the subject.

One time when I had Vicki's troop at Sandy Bend, I gave her and some fellow troop members a challenge as part of their cooking badge. They were told to fix chicken and dumplings for a troop meeting. That wouldn't have been too big of a problem because all three girls were good cooks. They were given money to buy the chicken and told that a neighbor near the camp had the chicken. The girls thought he had picked it up at the grocery store in Elizabeth but when they arrived at the farm, the farmer gave them a live chicken. Vic had made the arrangements ahead of time. After the initial surprise of being expected to kill the chicken, the girls rose to the occasion and did a good job.

My mother was a diabetic and had a heart condition. She was a frequent visitor and when she was unable to live alone she came to stay with us. The family made many adjustments and during the last two years of her life someone was always in the house with her. She had frequent bouts of chest pain and we never knew when her sugar would be out of balance.

Jean and Vicki could fix the special diet that was required and administer oxygen for shortness of breathe. Gayle combed her hair and Kelli played cards and watched TV with her. The relationship that my children had with their grandmother contributed to their outlook on life as adults. They learned to interact with people of all ages and be compassionate with those in need. It was a great loss when my mother died May 2, 1967 while I was taking her to the hospital in an ambulance.

In December, 1967 I developed a back problem and was hospitalized and placed in traction. I was allowed to come home for Christmas but returned the first part of January for surgery. I ordered finger foods and liquids that could be drunk through a straw from the hospital menu. I didn't want to be fed and since I wasn't permitted to raise my head, this type of diet worked out better. I went for a year without lifting anything heavier than a jug of milk and I used a long set of metal pick-ups to retrieve things from the floor.

When I came home after my first visit to the doctor after the surgery, I was greeted with, "Can you drive yet?" I hadn't realized how important my job as a chauffeur for teenage daughters was until then.

I went to work at our new community hospital in January, 1970. During the previous 14 years my time had been centered around the activities of four girls and keeping a household running. The work was a challenge because in a small hospital, employees are cross trained to work in many departments. I also worked all three shifts.

Jean had started to Alderson-Broaddus College in September and the extra income helped with tuition and other expenses. I was offered a job in a local family practitioner's office after I had been at the hospital two years. I decided to accept the offer because it meant all day shifts with Sundays and holidays off. I stayed there seven months and then went to work for another local physician, where I was to remain until June, 1986. I also worked one day each week at the State Health Department helping with evening clinics.

Vic and I decided to try and pay college expenses as they were due. To make for easier record keeping, we opened two accounts for each girl when they entered college. The Wirt County Bank account took care of living expenses and checks were written on the Traders Bank for anything concerning school. All of my pay checks from the Health Department were deposited in the Traders account. Plus, most of my earning from my regular job and a portion from Vic's check was funneled into educating our daughters for the next fourteen years.

Our children were good students and participated in many school and community activities. I had a standard answer when they would come to me and ask if they could try out for something or enter a contest. "You may, if you can loose like a lady." They usually achieved what they attempted and were gracious losers the few times they didn't win or place first.

I provided two majorette and one cheerleading uniform. When the last one left for college, we had five band instruments in the closet. I couldn't play any of them. The piano lessons I took from an elderly neighbor might have helped some if I had really wanted to play the saxophone or flute.

We listened to student council and class president speeches and the icing on the cake was when I heard the valedictory speech given by daughter #3 at graduation. I was also privileged to see Jean receive the God and Country award in Girl Scouting.

The custom of identifying our children by numbers originated when they would call home and I would get confused about which one I was talking with. They would say, "this is daughter #1, #2, #3, or #4" as a family joke.

I attended PTA and parent conferences at school. I was a band booster and worked the concession stand at ball games. I was sure that Gayle would get pneumonia from being out in the cold in her cheerleading outfit but she did fine and I learned to accept the fact that I wasn't going to be able to protect my children from all the unpleasant things in life.

We never knew what to expect from Kelli. For example, one day she became sick at school and decided to take a taxi home instead of calling me at work.

Another time she needed her birth certificate to register for basketball. She went to Gordon's Hospital where she was born and asked for it. They sent her to the courthouse.

She borrowed the 50 cents from one of the ladies in the County Clerk's office and went back to school with proof that she had been born.

When Kelli was eleven years old, she developed a high temperature and the doctors couldn't find a cause. She was tested for many things and one doctor thought she might have picked up some strange disease from a carnival worker during the Black Walnut Festival.

She was admitted to St. Joseph's Hospital in Parkersburg where her case was reviewed by all department heads. Finally, one of the doctors found a mass in her right side and an exploratory surgery was scheduled. The mass was removed and identified as an encapsulated appendix that was entwined around other organs.

She lost a lot of weight during her illness. I also sent her to a beautician who gave her treatments for hair loss due to the high fever. Kelli's school provided in-home tutors and she soon caught up with her class after missing three months of school.

I formed a close relationship with many of the patients I cared for while working in a doctor's office. The family practitioner had been in practice for several years and had a pleasant way with people. We treated the forth generation of some families. Part of my duties consisted of listening to people when they wanted to talk about problems they were having at home. I was often asked by young mothers for advice about their babies. I think they had confidence in my nursing skills, but mostly they trusted me because I had four children that were doing well.

The receptionist, cleaning lady and I were the only help in the office. His wife did the bookkeeping at home and worked in the office occasionally. Many of the patients were like an extended family and we scheduled appointments around what time the kids got off the school bus, golf games, bank directors meetings and the most important time in some of their lives was being home for their favorite soap operas.

We received many gifts of food but what we always looked forward to was Roxy's Christmas candy. I still cherish the tape of "Sweet Beulah Land" recorded by a patient's son. The practice was sold in June 1986 but I stayed on for a while until I went back to work at our community hospital.

Many changes had taken place since I had worked there 16 years before. There was a lot more paperwork as well as new technical skills. Nursing like most professions had different specialties. Even with my expertise as an office nurse I still needed to brush up on hospital routines. I took a re-entry course at St. Joseph's Hospital that was offered for nurses that hadn't worked for a while. My work hours were scheduled around the classes. I found the course to be enjoyable and helpful.

I worked in different departments of the hospital and finally settled to a regular schedule of working in the long term geriatric unit. Some of the patients had been there for many years and the staff became like a second family to them. I remained in that department until my retirement in 1996.

I might have worked for a while longer if Vic had not developed medical problems. Two days before Thanksgiving he went to his doctor for treatment of a sinus infection and during the visit the doctor suspected that he had an abdominal aneurysm and sent him to have x-rays. The doctor's diagnosis was confirmed and Vic was referred to a surgeon for surgery.

The operation was scheduled for December 18, 1995. He spent the next three weeks preparing for surgery with x-rays and blood tests. He gave two units of blood at the Red Cross to be used if needed. A chemical stress test showed some irregularities and a heart catheterization was ordered.

This was performed early Monday, December 18th and found there was enough blockage of the heart arteries to make it inadvisable to go on with the aneurysm surgery as planned.

One of our daughters came to Parkersburg Monday evening so she would be present for the aneurysm surgery the next morning. The game plan changed and she and I took her father to Charleston the next morning. Vic saw the heart surgeon and had a complete cardiac work-up.

Wednesday, December 20th, we sat in a large surgery waiting room for several hours with many other families. The stress of our wait was relieved somewhat when a surgical nurse that we knew from home, came in twice to report on Vic's condition.

The surgeon explained in a professional and kind manner that he had performed five by-passes and Vic was stable in intensive care.

We stayed in a motel conveniently located across the street from the hospital. On Christmas day I sat in Vic's room dressed in a Christmas shirt and Santa Claus hat. He progressed nicely and we brought him home December 26.

His greatest frustration came when he was told not to drive. Vic and I began the wait until the aneurysm surgery could be scheduled. There was less pre-surgery testing this time and Vic recuperated satisfactorily. He was able to give one unit of blood for surgery and four more units were donated by a nurse at the blood center, the doctor's receptionist, his niece, and his sister-in-law.

Vic was given a medical release and was scheduled for the operation for February 28, 1996. We checked into the hospital that morning and he left the room at 7 a.m.

Millie took off work and stayed with me in the waiting room. Vic was kept in the recovery room so that the surgeon could be nearby to monitor him closely between his other surgery cases. After ten hours we were told to go to the cardiac surgery waiting room. We waited there a while before I was permitted to see him.

I stayed with nearby relatives while Vic was in the hospital which was a big help. The drive to Spencer each day would have been an added worry due to the uncertain weather and road conditions. Vic's recuperation was slow but on May 2nd, all restrictions were lifted and the doctor told him that he could do anything that he felt like doing.

After his mother's death in 1992, we acquired part ownership of the farm and home where Vic grew up. We began to make improvements to the old house and my biggest contribution was removing plaster and lath boards from the walls. Four two-cubic-foot dumpsters were filled and hauled away to the landfill. At this writing we continue to work on the farm as a hobby.

I have always enjoyed reading and support our local library by placing memorial books when appropriate. In April 1996 I became involved in the Lauback Literacy volunteer program and became a tutor.

My daughter Gayle asked if I would tell her something about myself when I was younger. I have tried to recall what I thought might be of interest to her and her sisters. This is what launched my writing endeavors. I find pleasure in seeing words on paper and I enjoy "people watching". I think back to the story of my sister and brother announcing the birth of "Skinny Simmie" to the neighborhood. What a great story could have been written as they ran from house to house shouting "Mother has a black baby and she is ugly as sin."

Computer Basics-101
"Senior Style"

After months of waiting, I heard the jingle of the telephone. I picked it up and was greeted by an excited voice that said, "You all come. The Dynamic Duo from cyberspace has agreed to share their smarts with the first lucky ten on the waiting list."

This list had existed since word came from the politicians at the state capitol that they were providing computers for the old people that could make it to the senior centers in their community. A state employee that was up on this new fancy gadget would come and teach them how to visit with their grandkids by using something called e-mail.

The excitement of the chance to be educated fizzled out after the November election. We found out that a teacher for the class was just a joke to sway us to vote the right way.

The fact that we have a Committee On Aging leader that refuses to give up is why we now have a class. When she finally got someone to return a phone call, she was told, "Sorry lady, we can't help you." She swung into action and came up with a plan of her own.

I don't know what she did to make it happen, but on a Monday morning ten timid people filed into a room that had been transformed from a storage area to a classroom. There were tables along three walls that held cream-colored boxes that were bigger than a bread box and had a piece of glass on the front of them.

Some little kids had been playing in the room before we came and had left their A B C pieces on a tray in front of the boxes. These kids had not mastered the alphabet because not one bunch of letters was lined up right.

Two pleasant people greeted us and said, "Please be seated." From that moment, our life took on a new meaning. We were introduced to a thing that could be covered with your hand that had a ball on the bottom of it that helped it move around. A long wire like a tail extended from one end and it had two things that looked like fat piano keys that would go down when they were punched. The instructor assured us that the mouse would not hurt us and we would soon be the boss. We could make it do anything we wanted unless it got stubborn and decided to freeze.

Next we were told why the A B C's were mixed up. They were placed like that to make up what is called a keyboard.

With the patience of the Dynamic Duo we were soon throwing around terms like; font, bold, highlight, and delete. I went home one day wondering who named the floppy disc. I hadn't seen it move and not once did I see it flop around. It rests in its own special little slot and doesn't bother anyone.

I have considered this class a learning experience that I will long remember and it has been a pleasure to have met the Dynamic Duo, also known as Troy and Alma.

Writers By the Lakes

I paid the fee on Friday and was given a tag that entitled me to lunch in the big dining hall. While finishing my coffee, I checked my schedule, trying to decide where I wanted to spend the next two days. Would I listen to poetry, browse in the book store, or read my latest fiction creation to my fellow writers?

Two things were high on the list of things to do; Go to the banquet, and try to appreciate the gourmet meal while my thoughts were drifting to the assembly hall and the awards ceremony that was to follow. There would be a room full of people, all hoping this would be the night the world would be made aware of their great talent.

As I had read in the book of Matthew, "Many are called but few are chosen." Most writers would be left with the thought, "Oh well, maybe next year I'll get lucky and I'll be presented with a piece of paper that says 'You deserve to be mentioned with honor." I enjoyed the entertainment that was presented by those talented ones.

Then it was off to the bonfire at the camp circle or back to my room to check my schedule and regroup my thoughts to see how I could make the most of the remaining conference time.

I went for breakfast Sunday morning at an early hour.

The dining room was quiet; many had chosen to sleep "just 10 more minutes" before starting the day.

After the meal, as I walked down the lane, I saw a small wooden structure nestled at the edge of a lake. Curiosity drew me closer. I crossed a bridge and followed the path until I stood gazing at a small building. A seasoned conference goer sensed my look of wonderment and said to me, "This is the chapel. Please come in."

I walked up the steps and entered from the porch. Not knowing what to expect, I saw cathedral beams and rustic pews and I was engulfed in a feeling of complete peace as the inspirational readings were offered and voices blended with the music of the harpsichord. I knew that God was in our midst.

Morning greetings of the birds and ducks could be heard. As the sunlight filtered through the stained glass window, it cast reflections on the water below. I knew that "All things great and small are wonderful because the Lord God made them all."

I left at the close of the service inspired with the knowledge that this was truly the highlight of my conference experience.

Sweet Sixteen

"Hey Joanie, wait up" Barb shouted as she ran to catch up with her best friend. They were hurrying to make it to first period math class. Barb was waving a piece of the classified section of the morning paper that she had torn out before she left home.

She was a few months older than Joanie and was known among her teachers as a born leader. She liked to plan things and was excited about Joanie's birthday party that she was having in two weeks. "Read this, the part I circled," Barb said as she handed Joanie the paper. Joanie scanned the ad and said in almost a whisper, "Mom would freak out." Barb squealed, "Wouldn't it make your party one the gang would talk about for weeks?"

At the end of the school day the girls talked and decided that the ad would be Barb's present to Joanie, if she could change her mother's mind about having a cookout in the backyard.

Joanie was about to hit the milestone in her life when a girl turns 16. She wanted something special to remember it by. Her mother had been a single parent since her husband died when Joanie was five years old. She tried not to indulge her daughter and spoil her, but sometimes it was hard. She was saving money for Joanie's college expenses and she didn't think it was right to spend what it would cost to have a party that Joanie insisted all the kids have on their 16th birthday. She wanted the ballroom at the local hotel reserved and a four-piece band hired and the food catered by the hotel.

As Joanie was walking home from school she was thinking of the plan that she and Barb had thought about and knew she would have to compromise with her mother. As she hurried into the house she called out, "Mom, I'm home." "In here" Linda answered from the kitchen." How was school?" "Oh same old thing, nothing ever happens." Joanie said as shook her head and rolled her eyes to the ceiling.

"Mom, have you thought any more about my party?" "Yes Joanie, I have, and we can't afford what you would like. I'm sorry." "Could we have it at the hotel in one of the smaller banquet rooms?" Joanie asked in her most pleading voice. "We could take CD's for music and we could fix the food at home and take it."

Linda was surprised at her daughter's suggestion. Maybe she was more grown up than she thought. She turned to Joanie and said, "I think we can manage a party like that all right. I'll call the hotel and make the arrangements."

Joanie could hardly wait to call Barb and tell her that her mother had agreed to the alternate plan that they had talked about.

Excitement mounted as word got around among the kids who had been invited to the party and about the present that Barb was giving to Joanie.

Sixteen kids gathered at the hotel on the evening of the party. Joanie and her mother had compromised on the number of people they would invite. Joanie wanted to invite many more but her mother said the banquet room that had been rented couldn't possible hold everyone that she wanted to invite. She said she could invite sixteen, one for each year of her age.

Tension began to mount as the last present was opened. All the kids knew that Barb's present would be the highlight of the evening. Two girls looked at each other and giggled. Some of the crowd got up and began to walk around the room in nervous anticipation. Several of the kids had brought cameras. None of them knew how Barb planned to present her gift, but they were ready to find out.

Finally they heard a knock on the door. Barb ran and flung open the door and she couldn't believe what she saw. A hotel waiter stood there with a pink and white cake resting on a small cart. The cake was topped with a miniature plastic boy in a football outfit. "This isn't the cake I ordered," Barb said to the waiter.

Linda stepped from behind the waiter and said, "I began to get calls from parents asking what kind of party I was planning for my daughter, and did I know there was more to it than a live male model popping out of a cake? The deal included three other guys that danced around wearing swimming trunks or less."

"I checked with the Better Business Bureau and was told that the police had the group under surveillance. The group had made pitches at parties for young people. After they sang and danced for the kids, they offered them free alcohol and drugs, hoping they would get hooked. They had been fined and told to cease operation, but they couldn't resist the temptation to make one more haul before they moved onto another town."

Linda looked around the room and continued, "I canceled the order and the police have the group in custody. The officer that has been working on the case is here and would like to say a few words. Detective McIntyre, meet my daughter, Joanie, and her friends." As he looked at the group, he thought of his own teenage son.

"Kids, if you see something advertised that sounds too good to be true, it is probably a scam. I brought the ad from the paper and I'd like to read it for the ones who haven't seen it.""Let me make your party the talk of all your friends. Live model will pop up from a cake and provide entertainment. Call 1-800-555-1616 for details."

"I want to thank Linda and all the other parents for helping us catch those who prey on kids. That is all I have to say." He started toward s the door and then turned and said, "Good night kids. Have fun the rest of the evening."

Grandma's Summer Camp

As Harry pulled the model-A truck to a stop at the side of the old farm house, he was met by his sister Jenny. She was anxious to hear the news from town and see the county newspaper that he picked up at the post office when he made his weekly trip to town. She seldom went because there were too many chores to be done for both of them to go.

They lived far from the big cities but they had both read about "The Great Depression." They knew people sold apples on street corners and stood in bread lines. It was hard for them to imagine when they had so much. There was never a shortage of apples or peaches from the orchards and if they could beat the birds to the grape arbor they had plenty of grape juice and marmalade.

Harry had come to live with Jenny 20 years ago when her husband died as the result of an accident while he was cutting timber. Jenny was left with four children under the age of 10 to provide for.

She had managed to make a meager living with hard work and she was a good manager. Her three girls and one boy all had married and moved from the farm after finishing high school. One of the girls had worked her way through college and was now a teacher and one was a trained nurse. The other two had good jobs which Jenny was thankful for because many people couldn't find any kind of work.

Harry was tall with broad shoulders and a quick smile. When he was younger, he was considered a good catch by the young ladies of the community. His shoulders were now slightly stooped and his hair was beginning to gray. When he was asked why he never married, his answer was always the same. "I'm still waiting for the right gal to come along."

Harry handed Jenny a newspaper and a letter. She took them, tucked the letter in her apron pocket, and went into the house to read it at the kitchen table. One of the best times of the week was when Harry brought mail from one of her children. This letter today was from her oldest daughter, Jean. Jenny was hoping for news about the family highlight of the year. This was the time when they all got together at the end of what was affectionately known as "Grandma's Summer Camp".

The camp was a time when six grandchildren came to spend two weeks at the farm. The parents of the children took turns bringing them and this year it was Jean's turn.

Harry walked into the kitchen and put his packages on a side table. He looked at his sister and knew by the smile on her face that the letter contained the news they had been waiting for. "Well Sis, how much time do we have to get ready for the stampede?" He liked to sound as if he hated to see his nieces and nephews coming, but he was as excited as their grandmother was about the visit. Jenny looked up and said, "Jean says they will be here on the three o'clock bus this Friday."

For the past several years the parent whose turn it was to bring the group came on the bus with them. After helping load the kids in the truck and visiting with their mother a short while, they caught the next bus back home. Jenny always came with Harry to pick up the campers. She needed to get any instructions that had been sent by any of the parents about their children, things like who had the sniffles and might need some honey and lemon juice. She also enjoyed the short visit with whoever had brought the campers.

It was an excited bunch that climbed in the back of the truck as their uncle said, "Now you youngin's sit still and don't get up until we get home." As he put the tailgate of the truck up, Paul, a freckled faced twelve-year-old, said, "Don't worry Uncle Harry, I'll make sure they behave."

This was the first year for six-year-old twins, Ben and Becky, to come to Grandma Jenny's camp. They sat side by side quietly looking from Paul to their three other cousins.

Jenny had learned from experience that she couldn't handle more than six of her twelve grandchildren at one time and if they were younger than six she had problems with them being homesick.

Betty, Paul's ten-year-old sister, flipped her copper colored braids and gave her brother a scornful look. She didn't say what she was thinking because they had both promised their parents that they would try not to argue while they were at Grandma's house. Eleven-year-old Tom was taller than his cousin Paul and didn't have plans to be bossed around by him. Annie had long brown hair that her mother had trained to hang in curls by wrapping it in strips of rags before bedtime each night. Many of the family believed that the eight-year-old was a natural beauty. She had big brown eyes and dimples in her cheeks when she smiled. Some said she resembled Shirley Temple, the movie star.

Jenny and Harry had planned what they would do each day. They knew they had to keep the campers busy or they wouldn't want to come again. They both believed that the only way to do this was to plan ahead. The neighbors along the dirt road heard the campers coming before they saw the truck, because they were singing to the top of their voices.

When they pulled up in front of the house, Paul said, "You kids sit still until Grandma comes." Tom, Betty and Annie had been to camp and knew the rules, and Ben and Becky had been to visit with their parents and knew that a trip to the farm was always fun.

Jenny came around to the back of the truck as Harry was letting the tailgate down and said, "Everyone get your things and go sit on the front porch." The porch was built across the front of the house and extended around one corner toward the kitchen.

Jenny and Harry had made a two-week calendar on a piece of butcher paper and printed things in the blocks. At the bottom of the paper was what they liked to call reminders, not rules.

Paul, Tom and Ben would share a room on the second floor near Harry's room. Betty, Annie and Becky would have the back bedroom downstairs. Everyone was to be up and ready for breakfast at 7:00 a.m. and bedtime with lights out was set for 9:30 p.m.

Each morning the children were supposed to check the calendar to see what their job was for the day. The older kids knew they would all get a turn at helping in the kitchen, feeding the chickens, gathering the eggs, feeding Rover, the big collie dog and feeding Patches, the calico cat. This year she had a family of three kittens about a month old.

They would help in the vegetable garden, help Grandma in her flower beds that seemed to be planted everywhere, and help Harry in the barn. Jenny always said when asked why she had so many flowers, "They brighten things up and aren't much trouble."

Everyone was expected to keep their rooms and themselves clean. The younger ones might need a little help.

One thing the kids looked forward to was the surprise that was listed every other day on the calendar. They never knew what it would be until that morning at breakfast.

When they had completed their tasks for the day, they were free to climb trees, wade in the creek, or busy themselves with any games the group might think up. No one was supposed to go any place alone where they couldn't hear Grandma Jenny if she called.

The jobs were listed on the chart so that every child had a chance to try them all. When Paul helped Harry in the barn, his duties were different from Ben's. The six-year-old would ask endless questions and pet the animals.

His twin sister liked to work in the flower beds, but her Grandma Jenny had to make sure Becky knew the difference between a weed and a flower.

By the middle of the second week the surprises had included fishing in the creek, a ride on the hay wagon, picking blackberries, a hike to the apple orchard, and a picnic on Sunday with the family that lived on the adjoining farm. The campers never seemed to tire of swinging on the rope that Harry had tied in a tall oak tree.

One afternoon when the girls and Ben were playing jacks on the porch, Uncle Harry was snoozing in the hammock in the yard, and Grandma Jenny was knitting while she watched the game of jacks, Paul and Tom decided to try something they hadn't done before.

They had heard about Indians smoking peace pipes and both boys thought it would be great fun to try it. They took a pipe from the rack that was on the mantel in the parlor and Tom slipped it in the pocket of his overalls. They went across the yard and out the path that lead to the barn.

As they walked past the garden, they each pulled a handful of brown silk from the corn that was growing there. Paul had taken matches from the metal holder that hung on the kitchen wall. They sat on a bale of hay behind the barn and filled the pipe bowl with the corn silk.

Neither boy had dads that smoked a pipe but they had seen other men smoke and it didn't look too hard. Paul said he would be the big Indian Chief because he was the oldest, but Tom quickly reminded him that he was bigger so he should be the big chief. They finally came up with an idea. They would both be chiefs of different tribes.

Tom struck a match and held it to the bowl of the pipe. Nothing happened. Tom said, "Put it in your mouth and suck in. Maybe that will get it started." Paul did as his cousin instructed and then handed it to him. It was fired up and when Tom took a big breath in and his mouth filled with smoke. He began to cough and water ran from his eyes and nose. Paul said, "Give it back to me little baby." Tom gladly gave the pipe back to his cousin and watched as he put the pipe in his mouth and took a deep breath. Instead of showing the younger boy what a great chief he was, his face turned red and he began to choke. The pipe dropped from his mouth and Paul wondered if this is what people meant when they talked about someone "choking to death." By the time they had caught their breath both boys had decided they didn't want to be Indian Chiefs.

They wanted to get the pipe back in the house without anyone knowing it had been moved from the rack on the mantel. Tom picked the pipe up from the ground and said to Paul, "This thing is hot." Paul grabbed it from Tom and dipped it in the rain barrel at the corner of the barn. He said with a triumphant look on his face, "That will fix it." He wiped the pipe on his shirt tail.

As they approached the house their grandmother looked up from her knitting and said, "Where have you boys been?" They both answered at the same time, "No place, we were just walking around." They went upstairs to their room after putting the pipe back in the rack on the mantel.

Harry turned over in the hammock and called out, "Sis, I smell something, I think you are burning our supper." Jenny laid her knitting aside and with a skeptical look toward her brother said, "Harry, you better wake up. I'm not cooking anything. We are having sandwiches and today's surprise for supper."

The campers had been excited that morning when their Uncle Harry had announced they were going to make ice cream that evening.

Paul sat by the window in his bedroom completely absorbed in *The Adventures of Tom Sawyer*, when Tom yelled, "Look, smoke!" Paul looked up from his book and saw a swirl of grey smoke coming from behind the barn and said as he dashed across the room to the door, "Come on Tom. We have to tell Grandma." The boys ran through the house and out the front door yelling, "Grandma, the barn is on fire."

Harry started running toward the barn and Jenny began barking orders like a top army sergeant. "Paul, take this bucket, get some water from the pump and take it to your Uncle Harry. Tom, grab those brooms from the porch and head for the barn. Betty, you keep the little ones here."

When she reached the back of the barn, Harry was moving a smoldering bale of hay away from the barn with a pitchfork. Tom was beating the low flames in the grass with a broom, and Paul was dipping water from the rain barrel and throwing it around in all directions. Jenny saw that the fire was outside the barn and coming under control.

Harry leaned on the handle of the pitchfork and said in a halting voice, "It's out and we are lucky that the only damage is the barn door is scorched and, we lost a couple bales of hay."

Jenny looked around and said, "I can't imagine what happened. We never leave a lantern in the barn with oil in it." Harry looked at Jenny and said, "Sis, you don't suppose that one of those hobos that travel around the country slept in the barn last night and had something to do with the fire starting?" "I don't think so, they always come to the kitchen door and ask for a handout first." Jenny answered.

Tom looked puzzled and said, "Uncle Harry, what is a hobo?" Harry looked at Tom and said, "Son, they are men that are down on their luck and don't have a home. They ride trains across the country and stop and work a few days on a farm or for people who live near the railroad for food or small wages. They don't stay in any one place very long."

Paul was thinking of the peace pipe and had a feeling that the two Indian Chiefs might have had something to do with the fire. Jenny said, "Harry, would you mind driving into town and asking the sheriff if he has seen any strangers around?" Harry started to the house and said, "I'll go as soon as I wash the black off my face and get some of the hay out of my hair."

Paul and Tom whispered to each other as they followed their grandmother to the house. Paul said, "Do you think we should tell them that we had the pipe and dropped it on the ground when it got hot?" Tom answered, "Maybe, but what if the sheriff comes and takes us to jail?" "He doesn't know we have done anything wrong." Paul reasoned with his cousin. But Tom felt scared and said, "Lawmen are smart, especially sheriffs."

They continued to talk and as they saw Harry getting into the truck, Paul said, "Uncle Harry, Tom and I want to tell you something." When they had finished their story, Harry said, "Boys, I think we better have a talk with your grandmother." They walked back to the porch and Harry said to his sister, "Jenny, come, into the kitchen we want to talk with you. The rest of you kids play in the yard." Jenny looked at her brother as she got up from her chair. What could be wrong? He sounded so serious.

The four of them sat down around the kitchen table and Harry said, "These young men have something to tell you." While Paul and Tom related their story, their grandmother looked straight ahead and sat quietly with her hands folded on the table. When they finished Paul said, "We're sorry we burned the barn door and ruined the bales of hay." Tom spoke up saying, "Really Grandma, we just wanted to pretend like we were Indian Chiefs."

Tears dropped on her cheeks and she seemed to be talking to herself when Jenny said, "I promised John before he died that I would take good care of his pipe, even had Harry make a special rack for it so it could have a place of honor on the mantel in the parlor. I never let my son have his dad's pipe when he was a little boy. I was afraid he would drop it." Jenny looked at the boys and continued in a sad voice, "To think of how I have protected and cherished that pipe all these years it is hard for me to believe that it was stolen, stuffed with corn silk and dipped in a rain barrel."

Harry had slipped from the kitchen and brought the pipe back from the parlor. He knew that through the years when things were not going well or one of the children was sick his sister would go to the parlor and say, "I need some time alone to think how John would have handled this problem." He hadn't realized until today how much the pipe meant to her or why she always chose the parlor to do her thinking..

Paul and Tom sat fidgeting and looked like they might cry at any moment. Harry said, "I'll clean the pipe and make sure all the water is out of the stem."

Jenny suddenly knew she had to deal with the present situation and said, "Thanks Harry. You boys need to learn to have respect for other people's property. To help you think about what you did, I want you to help your Uncle Harry fix the barn door, and tonight after supper while the rest of the family is making homemade ice cream, you can stay in your room."

Paul and Tom had been at the farm when ice cream had been made and knew how good it tasted. Tonight they not only wouldn't get any to eat, they would miss the fun of helping get the ice from the ice house and turning the crank while salt and ice was being added around the can. As they left the kitchen, they knew Grandma's punishment was fair. They worried more about what would happen to them when their parents found out what they had done.

That evening Paul and Tom sat by the window in their room and listened to the four other campers as they laughed and took turn turning the crank of the ice cream freezer. They had been sent to their room as soon as they finished supper. They had offered to help get ice in the wheel barrow from the ice house, but they were told by their grandmother that their help was not needed.

The next two days were spent getting ready for the family gathering when more than twenty people would come to visit and hear about Grandma's camp.

After Harry had gone to town and bought lumber to replace the barn door, Paul and Tom were kept busy as his helpers. The other kids knew there had been a fire but they didn't know what roll their older cousins had played in it. Jenny had handled the situation like she had with her own children. If a child was being punished, it was their decision to talk about it or keep it to themselves. Paul and Tom had chosen to keep the Indian Chief caper a secret between the two of them.

When the last coat of red paint was being put on the barn door Saturday morning, with a worried look Tom said to Paul, "Do you think Grandma will tell?" "I don't know. We will just have to wait and see." Paul answered his younger cousin.

Jenny's children and their families had all arrived by noon. Everyone brought food to add to what their mother had on hand. The afternoon was spent by each person checking out things around the farm that they wanted to see. There wasn't a schedule like Jenny used for her campers, although she did like for people to be together for meals.

That evening while Jenny was sitting on the porch listening to the conversation of the others, her son John said, "Mom, I see you decided to spruce up the barn by painting one of the barn doors." Paul was in the yard and waited for his grandma's answer. Jenny said, "Yes, seems like something always needs fixed."

The next afternoon when the people were getting ready to leave for home, Paul and Tom told their grandmother they wanted to show her something. She followed them into the parlor and after shutting the door they both hugged her at the same time and said, "We love you. Why didn't you tell anyone about the pipe? We are sorry we caused the fire and we are really sorry that we bothered Grandpa's pipe. We didn't know it meant so much to you."

Their eyes were fixed on the pipe on the mantel as Paul said, "We never met Grandpa, but I'm sure he was braver than any Indian Chief." Jenny gathered both boys close and said, "I'm sure your grandpa would have forgiven you and would have been satisfied for this to be our little secret."

Each boy went home with their parents that day knowing that they had learned a lesson that would be with them for the rest of their lives. Their Grandma Jenny was a special person and they both agreed that she would make the smartest and bravest lady Indian Chief, if she ever decided to join a tribe and close Grandma's Jenny's Summer Camp.

Wanted 9-5 Job,
Retirement is Too Exhausting

I entered the work force at the age of 14 as a kitchen helper in a restaurant. Retirement was the last thing I was thinking about. My goal in life was to earn enough money to purchase a vest type sweater like some of my friends had.

The going rate for someone of my experience was 25 cents an hour, and by the time I had earned enough money for the sweater, it didn't seem that important. Besides the fad then was brown and white saddle oxford shoes.

I learned to adjust to the ups and downs of adolescence and went on to lead a productive life as an adult. I thought, "I had been there and done that," until suddenly it was time to think about retirement and applying for social security.

The big day finally arrived when I said good-by to my fellow workers at the nursing home where I had worked for the past 25 years. On Friday afternoon there were cake, punch and good wishes from the staff. I think I was supposed to cry in the punch and choke on the cake, but tears just wouldn't come. I turned my time card in to the personnel manager and left with a feeling of being free as a bird with the chance to explore new adventures and to sleep past 5:30 in the morning.

I would miss most of the people that I had worked with over the years, but it would be a blessing not to have to face some of them every day.

The following Monday morning I was in my favorite chair checking Ann Landers' column to see what problems she was solving today. I had awakened at an early hour and gotten up after turning and tossing in a futile effort to go back to sleep. I realized that my body would have to adjust to the luxury of living without an alarm clock.

Living in a small town has many advantages, but having a private life is not on the list that the Chamber of Commerce sends out to lure new people to the community. Word had spread like wild fire that I had quit work and would be a good candidate to volunteer for all the things that needed to be done in town.

The first caller wanted me to come to the Brownie Scout meetings on Tuesday after school for the next six weeks and teach the little girls how to make cookies. She went on to explain that I could use the kitchen in the church where the troop met and all the ingredients would be donated by the girls' mothers. Most of the mothers work and don't have time to devote to teaching culinary skills. The lady rambled on and I finally interrupted her and said that I had other plans.

She said the committee would be disappointed. They had chosen me because I now had so much free time and knew I would do a good job because I was a grandmother. Why do people think that all grandmothers are cookie experts? My last chocolate chip adventure was a total disaster. The cookies stuck to the pan and crumbled when I finally pried them loose.

I was watching the morning news show on television with my second cup of coffee when the phone rang again. It was the secretary from the water department. She offered me the "privilege" to serve the community by collecting names on a petition to upgrade the town's sewer system. I declined with the excuse that I had made plans to visit a friend and I would be out of town. I didn't have plans to do anything, but if the phone kept ringing, I would think of something.

They must have been desperate because two hours later another woman from the same office called and said they had failed to mention that the petition wasn't due for two weeks and felt sure I would reconsider. I assured her I was busy and said no again.

I decided after lunch to go to the grocery store and see what it was like to shop without bumping buggies with the after work crowd. It was true the aisles weren't as crowded and parking was not a problem, but I picked the same time to shop as the president of the day care center.

She stopped me at the diary case as I was checking the dates on the cottage cheese cartons. She explained that at the last meeting of the day care committee, it was unanimously decided to ask me to read to the children at story time. They knew I would enjoy it because my grandchildren lived out of state and I would have lots of free time since I retired.

I edged my cart toward the produce counter as I told her I hadn't decided what I wanted to do with my afternoons and not to count on me. She seemed surprised, but I smiled and continued my journey up one aisle and down another. By the time I had reached the check out station, I had made up my mind that I would rather spend my time reading a romance novel than sitting on the floor reading to a circle of four year olds.

Having lived in a small town for the past 35 years, I had no desire to move when I retired. I had a handle on the mechanics of day to day living.

I knew the doctor, lawyer, pharmacist, librarian, preacher, and the undertaker all by first names. I also knew 80 percent of the town people and had a nodding acquaintance with the other 20 percent. If something went wrong with the washer or refrigerator that you recently bought, you knew exactly who to tell your troubles to. Bill or Joe at the hardware store would "make it right." There was no need to call out of town and talk to an answering machine about your leaky washer and try to explain the problem by pressing numbers on the telephone dial.

I was asked by someone from the 20 percent of the population that I knew casually if I planned to move close to my children when I retired. Our children grew up in this town and almost everyone knows they are scattered across the country. The only way we could live close to our children would be to have a camper and pull it into their driveway and park until it was time to move on to the next child's house. That doesn't sound like much fun. I've decided to stay put and visit occasionally.

I have heard retired people talk about hitting an emotional low after they had done all of the little jobs they wanted to do, but never found time while they were working. Their life seemed to come to a halt after all the recipes were typed and put in order, all the drawers and closets cleaned and the grandchildren's pictures put in albums with clever little captions written under each one.

Some became so bored that a trip to the grocery store was the highlight of their week. I left the workplace that last day with one thought in mind, tonight I won't have to set the alarm clock. I'll worry about being depressed later. I thought about giving the clock to the Salvation Army thrift store, or having a ceremony and retiring it to a shelf in the attic. I'm glad I didn't. I plan to use it to help me get to important things on time like my exercise group or the class for beginner computer operators.

The next week I decided to apply for social security benefits. I drove to the office building and after the third try I

111

finally wrestled my car into a tight parking space between a Ford Escort in front and a Dodge pickup behind me. The parking meter had a 60 minute limit and after digging to the bottom of my purse, I dutifully fed the meter.

I entered the big building thinking about meeting my friend at the mall for lunch at noon and then some shopping. It was now 9:30. I would have plenty of time. How long could it take to tell the clerk my name and address and that I wanted to apply for social security?

I hurried through the second set of glass doors as I heard someone yell, "Number seven." I thought I had made a mistake and walked into an auction house. The room was crowded and everyone had a white plastic card with a black number on it. The cards were about as big as the frames I had on my desk at home that my grandchildren's pictures were in. I hadn't been to many auctions, but I thought after number seven bought the last item that the auctioneer would put something else on the block immediately. From the back of the room I was able to see the clerk or cashier talking to a woman at the front of the room. I thought she must be number seven and they were collecting the money for what she bought.

As I started to leave to check the directory in the main entrance, a young man looked at me and said, "Aren't you even going to get a number and wait a while?" I explained to him that I was looking for the social security office and didn't have time to stay for the auction today. He smiled and said, "Lady, this is the social security office and you need a number. Wait here and I'll get you one." He proceeded to make his way through the crowd as people gave him dirty looks and mumbled words that I couldn't hear, but I'm sure they weren't kind. When he came back, he seemed pleased with himself as he handed me a card with number twenty-three on it. He said, "My name is Cal and this number gives you a place in line like at a donut shop. I got in line at 8:30

this morning. I wanted to be one of the first in when the doors opened at 9:00. I got number 12 but the clerk that is working on my disability case won't be in the office until 10:00, but I'm not surprised. I've been here so many times that I've gotten used to waiting."

He looked big and strong and I wondered why he was there. He must have read my thoughts because he went on to explain, "I've got a bad back. I hurt it a couple of years ago on a construction job, and I've been trying to get help ever since. Three different doctors have checked me and they can't agree on what to put on the health forms. One older doctor said there must be something I could work at. He said maybe I should go back to school and learn something besides ditch digging. I sure don't want to go back to school again. I swore I'd never go back when I got out on my 16th birthday."

Cal continued on about his wife and three kids, but I heard a word only now and then because I had become engaged in one of my favorite pastimes–people watching. I had often done this in an airport. There you can let your imagination run wild with such questions as how many people will pass you with a piece of luggage on wheels in 10 minutes, or how many people will walk on the wrong side of the moving walkway. The game possibilities are endless and the time between flights soon melts away.

This situation would have to be approached differently in this crowded room with everyone aiming for the same goal. They wanted someone with authority to listen to their problems and needs.

I decided to play the counting game first. I discovered that there were sixteen other people with cards, 15 people who had come to keep their friends company, seven preschoolers and two babies in strollers. This was as close as

I was going to get to knowing how many were waiting with me.

The room was buzzing with activity. A little boy was chasing his sister around the chairs that were bolted to the floor in two neat rows. Their mother was yelling for them to stop, but they knew she wouldn't come after them and take a chance of losing her seat. They quieted down when a lady distracted them with an offer of breath mints that she had fished from a big shopping bag.

Two men who appeared of retirement age were having a heated exchange of words about the merits of the government, "Sending all that money overseas, and wanting to cut the social security checks of people who had worked hard all their lives." They were in mutual agreement that they shouldn't have to help support the dead beats who were too lazy to work.

I was glad I had worn low heel shoes. It made the wait easier as I leaned against the wall. I was silently betting against myself as to how long the baby would sit in the stroller without crying. My first guess was five minutes and the second ten minutes. Both of my projections were wrong, because the little boy started fussing and trying to climb out of the stroller in less than three minutes.

The situation grew more intense when the mother searched the diaper bag and discovered she had left her son's bottles in the car. A lady who had come with her was sent to the car which was parked two blocks down the street in search of the bottles. People were looking at the mother as if it were her fault that the kid continued to scream at the top of his voice.

At that time I remembered a rule that I had been taught in Sunday School when I was a child. When you pray for something, it should always be followed by a "thank you." I decided to give it a try. "God please let that woman have the right key to the car and get that bottle back here on the double, and thank you for letting me live through similar experiences when my kids were little."

A few people had been called by 10:30 a.m. I had gotten a seat and the clerk was talking with number 15. Cal had been called before he finished telling me his life story. I guess I'll never know why the government was giving him such a hard time about sending him a monthly check and providing other benefits.

The lady who I was seated next to must have been in the office before because she was prepared for a long wait. She worked on her check book, addressed envelopes and then settled in to read Norman Vincent Peale's book The Power of Positive Thinking. I thought, "There is one person who will be able to state her case when her number is finally called."

The room remained crowded because as people left others drifted in. It was 11:15 when number 21 was called. I felt elated, just two more to go and it would be my turn.

I was in the back of the room and couldn't imagine what was happening when I heard a chorus of moans followed by "Oh no!" The people in the front of the room told the rest of us that the clerk said they were short of help today because someone had called in sick and the desk would be closed for lunch.

It was 11:30, and for a fleeting moment I thought about leaving and then I realized that I had two hours of waiting behind me. I was near the top of the list, so I decided to hang in there.

I was bored with "people watching." I liked to read but all I saw were some government pamphlets on "How to File Your Income Tax" and "How to Plan for Retirement" and I realized I didn't really care. I would think about that another day.

I sat there and envied the woman who had been smart enough to bring along Dr. Peale for company. My adrenalin started to pump when the clerk came back and called number 22. A man walking with a cane and the aid of a young lady at his side made his way to the desk and began to tell the clerk how long he had been waiting before he told her what he wanted.

I was rehearsing in my mind what to say when I finally reached the magic chair in front of the clerk when someone tapped me on the shoulder and said, "What number do you have?" At the same time the clerk asked, "Did number 23 leave?" I jumped up and made my way to the front of the room, my moment had arrived. I explained that I would soon be 65 and wanted to apply for social security.

She typed my social security number into the computer and looked puzzled. She informed me that the necessary form had been mailed to me two months ago and all that I needed to do was to complete them and mail them to the address provided. If I had questions there was an 800 number at the bottom of the page that I could call.

I tried to think, but couldn't imagine what she was talking about unless the forms came and I had pitched them in with the junk mail for recycling. I had waited two and one-half hours for this! In addition, I had a friend at the mall who would probably never speak to me again.

I left the crowd and after taking care of my parking ticket, I went home to rummage through my desk and the recycling bin and wondered if all the steps to retiring were to follow this same pattern . . . .

A Cherished Moment

Dear Aunt Martha,

I want to share the happy time Tom and I had while visiting with the families of Sally and Bob last week. We enjoyed seeing the grandchildren and we talked for hours about things that had happened in the past. It was a fun and relaxing time.

Nothing could have prepared us, for the surprise we experienced when everyone met at Sally's house for dinner. As Tom and I entered the front hall, we heard music as we stepped into a cluster of golden bells hanging from the ceiling. The number fifty hung from the bottom of each bell. I tried to grasp what was happening. I looked to the left and saw a banner that said HAPPY 50th ANNIVERSARY hanging across the windows. On another wall hung three wreathes with 50 imprinted in the center of each one.

Sally's son, David, was at the piano playing Wedding March from Midsummer Night's Dream. Throughout the evening he played other selections in the background. The dining room table was set with a white cloth and gold wedding bands were linked to form napkin rings. A vase of pink irises rested on the end of the table. My favorite candy during my teen years was Hershey Almond bars and a dish of miniature gold bars tied with white anniversary ribbon completed the table decorations.

Next we were served a meal fitting for a king and queen, which I think we were for a few hours that evening.

After dinner the table was transformed into the beautiful, glittering, focal point of the evening. A lace tablecloth was placed over an under cloth of gold and tiny wedding bells adorned with the number 50 were scattered around the table.

A white cake topped with a heart edged in delicate lace with a gold 50 in the center was placed near the flower vase. Gold wedding bands on the edge of the cake helped to make it a true work of art. Cutting the cake brought back fond memories of our first wedding reception that you so lovingly planned.

I finally realized that our family had tried to re-create the reception we had so many years ago. I could tell you had helped Sally with the plans when she visited you in the nursing home at Christmas time.

Aunt Martha, I can never tell you what your love and care meant to a frightened and lonely twelve year old girl after the death of her parents in the accident. When the judge gave you custody of me and my older sister, it was a new beginning for us. I soon learned that he had made the right decision.

Bob and Sally were fortunate to have you as a grandmother figure over the years. They learned so much from you and are now happy and contented with their lives.

Say hello to your roommate, Edna and I'll see you after we return home.

Your devoted niece,

Francine

Happy Birthday to Me

The celebration continued from the time I heard a footstep on the porch until I stood and waved to the big silver car as it drifted down Capehart Street 40 hours later.

Those hours were packed with an unbelievable array of fun and games. I visited a shoe store and selected a perfect pair of AVIA walkers. I had a Chinese gourmet meal that consisted of many things, rice being the only thing I really could pronounce. Some talented person exchanged a thesaurus book by using the internet because I said bigger print would be more suited to my bifocals.

Daughter #5 presented me with a wood carving and spent the evening helping me enjoy my lemon cheese birthday cake.

The mouse did double duty as technicians coaxed it to perform a series of things to celebrate my special day. The poem I had written for my grandson Andrew was enhanced with the art work they added.

Daughter #4 was chosen to spend the day with her father while #2 and #3 had the privilege of escorting me to a most unusual wedding. While Daughter #4 helped measure dirt in the Earth Box to make a home for broccoli plants, we ventured to a new experience.

Playing the heavy as mothers sometimes like to do, I was urging us on with statements like, "We have to be seated in the church 30 minutes before the ceremony starts and park the car so we won't get blocked in."

The church was on a small bank surrounded by spring flowers and pale green leaves were beginning to emerge from the trees that could be seen in the background.

The bride was attired in a traditional long white wedding gown. Guests were dressed in a variety of styles and each one depicted the love they felt for the bride and groom.

The cousin of the bride hosted a reception at his place of business. He reserved the dining area for the wedding guests. A lovely buffet table was set. The wedding cake and a bride and groom table with champagne added to the decor. Many pictures were taken near the spot where Hank Williams Sr. once performed.

On the way home I was treated to a Happy Meal from McDonald's. A small pink change purse was my prize that came with the meal. That was my first experience of getting a meal in a sack that was meant for a little kid.

Talents of my daughters know no end. That evening they helped install an air conditioner in the computer room. Our pillows now have anti allergy covers.

Wal-Mart stock showed a rise as we went back and forth. I don't think anyone kept count of the number of times we covered that half mile. I consider a Wal-Mart visit one of life's little added pleasures.

Daughter #1 was as close as Verizon could get her. I enjoyed talking with her and describing the happenings of this fun bunch.

The Cat in the Hat card said it all. "Happy Birthday to Me." What more can I add, except that I cherish my Playmate Pal Cooler. The label says it will hold nine cans or seven quarts. I plan to tuck all the memories of my special day in it and carry it with me for years to come.

Peppermint Sticks and Banana Peels

"Gary, have you seen my mother and Austin, the sky is getting dark and I don't want them out in the storm?" Gary looked at his next door neighbor as she ambled along the sidewalk that ran by the trailers in the park. He was in his wheelchair on the porch and couldn't go to her, so he called out, "No I haven't."

He thought about what he should do and decided that calling Mr. Bosley, the park owner, was all that he could do. He knew that Rachel was quiet and kept to herself and he wondered if she should be living alone and driving a car.

It was last week that Sandy, a lady that lived across the street, had to back Rachel's car out of a neighbor's yard when she had attempted to drive two blocks up the street to the trash dumpster.

Gary knew that three-year-old Austin came to visit sometimes, but his grandmother always brought him and he thought if Rachel's mother were living she would surely be over 100 years old. It didn't add up. Something was wrong.

Gary was a diabetic and had recently had his right leg amputated above the knee. He spent his days in a wheelchair but was glad that he could care for himself with help from his mother and brother. This was the first time since surgery that he had felt like he could be helpful to anyone.

He watched Rachel for a while and then turned his wheelchair and went up the door ramp into his living room. He dialed Mr.Bosley and told him that he was worried about Rachel. He looked out the window and saw her sitting on her porch looking up and down the street like she expected to see someone coming.

Ed came as soon as Mr.Bosley called and as he entered the trailer he saw his mother sitting in her recliner with a worried look on her face. "Mom, what's wrong with you?" "Ed, I'm worried about my mother and Austin being caught in a storm. I tried to tell her she shouldn't take him for a walk, but she wouldn't listen. She said, 'A little rain never hurt any one.'"

Ed tried to stay calm, because he knew that getting excited could trigger an asthma attack and make breathing hard for him. He walked with a cane due to a hip injury he had received as a result of a car wreck five years ago. He lived alone about ten miles from his mother and helped her as much as his health permitted.

"Mom, Grandma has been dead for thirty years, and Austin is home playing with his kitten." Rachel looked at her sixty-year-old son and said, "You've always been a good boy, so don't start lying to me now."

Ed didn't know what to do, he knew his mom had a tendency to forget things now and then, but he had never faced anything like this. He decided not to argue with her and said, "Mom, I think they will be O.K., the clouds have left and the sun is trying to shine."

The worried look seemed to melt away from Rachel's face and she began to talk to her little poodle that had jumped up in the chair beside her. "FeFe, Ed has come to see us, isn't that nice?"

Ed knew he had to get out of that trailer before his mother saw the tears he was trying to hold back. "Mom, I have to go now, are you sure you are all right?" "Why Ed, FeFe and I are just fine, what made you think we weren't?" "Call me when you have time."

Ed picked up his cane and made his way to his truck. He didn't know what he should do next, but knew he needed some time alone to think.

Two days later he wasn't any closer to getting things sorted out about his mom. She was the strong one of the family and had managed fine since the death of his father 15 years ago. She was the one he looked to for support when his daughter had heart surgery. Later when his marriage had failed, she didn't offer any advice, but was a willing listener when he needed to talk. Thoughts were spinning around in his head, but the same question kept coming back again and again. "What am I going to do, what can I do?" There seemed to be no solution.

The glare from the sun shining on the new fallen snow made Josh's eyes smart as he rode along the road to the county seat.

He had been in the saddle since early morning and he was anxious to get home to Becky and the kids. When he was elected assessor three years ago, he didn't know all that he would be called on to do.

The snow was to be expected with Christmas less than two weeks away and it was a welcome sight to all the kids. They were sure Santa could travel easier in his sled with snow on the ground.

He saw the steeple of the courthouse as he reached the top of the hill. He knew it wouldn't be long until he finished what he had to do and he could be on his way home.

He tethered Dobbin to the hitching rail and walked up the front steps of the courthouse. "Hey John," he said as he entered the county clerk's office, "I got another citizen's name for you to write in that big book of yours."

John looked up as he pushed his glasses up on his nose. "Why Josh I haven't seen you in a spell, I suppose you been out looking at farms and cattle to see how many taxes you can make people pay."

John smiled at his friend and said, "That's only part of my job, I also have to count the new babies when Dr. Flannery isn't there for the birthing. When grandmas or a neighbor delivers the baby, they have no way of getting the information to the courthouse until someone comes to town. That is usually me or the circuit riding preacher."

"Charlie and Sairy Bonnett from over on Nobe Ridge had a girl born October 12th and named her Rachel Ruth." He handed John a scrap of paper, I wrote down what I thought you need to record it.

"Thanks Josh, I'll get little Rachel's name copied right away, but you'll have to wait a few years to assess her for taxes." Rachel became an official citizen that day, but no one could have predicted what was in a store for her in the years to come.

Rachel looked at her big sister Zada and wondered why she was crying. The sun was shining brightly as they bounced along the dirt road in the back of the wagon. The tracks on the road were uneven and there were big holes from the recent spring thaw.

Rachel had been excited that morning when she heard her dad say, "Sairy, get the kids ready and you can ride to the store with me." In all her five years she had never been for a ride in the wagon except the time that Grandpa Tom had let her and Zada ride with him when he went to the upper meadow to gather chestnuts.

Rachel's mom hustled around and dressed her, Zada and baby Joey in their best clothes for the three-mile trip. In case any of the neighbors from the surrounding farms had come to pick up their mail or get supplies, she wanted them to look their best.

Rachel and Zada sat in the back of the wagon on some feed sacks and their mom sat up front with Joey on her lap. Zada seemed happy enough to Rachel until they started home.

They had both been amazed when they entered the store. Men were sitting around the pot bellied stove in the center of the room. Rachel couldn't figure out why, because there wasn't any fire burning in it. They were chewing tobacco and trying to spit into a spittoon at the side of the stove. They seemed to be missing it most of the time.

The men looked up as they entered the store and Zada and Rachel hid behind their mother's skirt. One man said, "Hi Charlie, I see you brought the woman and youngin's with you today." He answered, "Sairy needed to get some calico to make Zada some clothes. She is growing like a weed and can hardly get into some of her dresses, but there is a lot of good wear left in them for Rachel."

The trip to the store was Rachel's first adventure away from the farm. She gazed from one thing to another. There were shelves with bright colored cloth. Barrels of pickles and things she didn't recognize in other containers lined up in front of the counter. Big glass jars were filled with licorice sticks, horehound drops, and peppermint pieces. One smaller jar contained red-hot cinnamon drops.

She had seen candy at home when her dad had it, and last Christmas Aunt Blanche brought her and Zada a sack of peppermint sticks.

Many of the people were buying seeds because it was almost planting time. Rachel saw hoes and shovels and some tools that she hadn't seen before.

When her parents had done their storin', Rachel and Zada climbed back in the wagon and they were soon on their way home. Zada was two years older than Rachel and had been more aware of what had been bought in the store. She was sobbing and said, "I wanted one but there all gone." Her mother said, "Hush Sissy and you can have a biscuit and jelly when we get home."

Rachel looked up to the front of the wagon where the peels from a bunch of bananas lay on the floor. At meal time her father always ate what he wanted and her mom and the kid got what was left. Zada thought she would get a banana because it was a special day with the trip to town and mom getting yard goods to make her a new dress. Rachel didn't cry because she hadn't seen the bananas, and even if she had she had reasoned that things like that were only for her dad.

Rachel was always glad to see Grandpa Tom ride up to the front gate on his big brown horse Susie. Most of the time he was on his way to some church to hold a meeting, but he always took time to visit and tell her and Zada a story.

Sometimes he read from the big black book that he carried in his saddle bags. Sairy was pleased when he had time to stay for dinner. She seldom had company and it was a treat to hear the news of all the people on his circuit.

Rachel didn't realize what an important person her grandpa was until she started to school and heard the other kids talking. There were eight grades in one room and the ages of the children ranged from six years to teenagers.

One day at recess she heard a group of big girls talking and giggling about Dave and Bill Wolfe being so handsome. The conversation suddenly stopped, when they saw Zada and her. They were walking toward the rope swing that hung from the big oak tree at the edge of the playground.

Rachel was surprised when SueEllen said to the group, "It's a shame for those Bonnett kids to have such a dad, when their granddad is so nice." Janie added to the conversation by saying, "My mom says he is the laziest man on the face of the earth and he ran thru with all the things his father gave him when he was married." Not to be outdone, Ella Mae said, "Did you know that Reverend Bonnett had five kids and he gave them all a piece of land, a cow, a team of horses, and $100 when they married?"

"All the kids have done fine except Charlie. He won't work the farm and they wouldn't even have a garden if his wife didn't plant it. He has sold off most of the land and my pa says he is about to pull up stakes and move to another county."

Rachel and Zada had heard everything the girls had said, but they didn't understand it. They didn't have time to think about it because Miss Conley began ringing the bell to let everyone know that recess was over. They hurried because they knew if you were late you had to stand in the corner and all the kids starred at you. Rachel would ask her mother that evening why the big girls were saying things about their family.

That evening after supper Rachel's dad was in his favorite chair on the porch, and her mother had gone to feed the chickens and milk the cow. She and Zada had been left to wash the dishes. Rachel looked at her sister with a troubled expression and said, "Do you think those girls at school were right when they said we were going to move?" Zada said, "I don't know, but we'll ask mom when she brings the milk in."

Rachel was hanging the dishrag on the rack, when her mother entered the kitchen to strain the milk and put the eggs in the basket on the shelf. She ran to her mother and said, "Mommie, Ellie Mae Walker told some of the girls at school today that we're moving; are we really?" Rachel blurted this all out so fast that her mother just looked at her for a moment before she answered. "Well girls, your dad has been thinking on it, but it depends on whether he can find anyone to buy the farm and house."

The farm was in poor condition with the meadows overgrown with brush and the cornfields hadn't been planted since the family moved there eight years ago. It would be hard to find a buyer.

Two months later as the sun was coming up Rachel and her family were on their way to a little town twenty miles over in Monroe County. Her dad had sold the farm for about half its value to Glen Master whose farm joined theirs. Glen's farm was one of the best in the county. He saw it as the perfect chance to add to his acreage.

The horse, cow, chickens, and all the garden tools had been sold along with the house and farm. Rachel's dad said, "We won't need them because I have bought a store."

It was late at night when they pulled up to a grey building with a big window in front. Rachel and Zada climbed down from the wagon their dad had hired from Seth Barton to move them to their new home. "Well Charlie, I'll help you unload my wagon and be starting back.", Seth said.

His sister lived a couple miles out of town and he planned to spend the night with her.

They all had to help carry things and it was then that Rachel realized they were going to live in three rooms in the back of the store. Her mom finally saw how tired she and Zada were after making several trips from the wagon to the store, and said, "Girls get you a quilt and lay down on that straw tick in the corner." Rachel was soon asleep and forgot everything until she heard her dad say, "Sairy don't you have that coffee ready yet?"

After living in the country, Rachel found life in a small town interesting. They had moved at the end of the school term. She had adjusted to living in a smaller house and Zada and she had made some new friends with kids that came in the store with their parents. Little Joey would soon be two years old and was an active little boy.

Rachel was puzzled when Aunt Blanche came one day and said she was going to stay for a while. She wondered where everyone would sleep.

Aunt Blanche was Sairy's oldest sister and was a favorite of her nieces. She was tall and thin and her smile and the twinkle in her eyes seemed to say she enjoyed life. That evening after the store was closed, Aunt Blanche asked Rachel and Zada if they would like to go camping with her. They didn't know what camping was but it would be fun if their aunt was there. She began to gather quilts, pillows and a piece of clothesline. She looked at us and said, "Girls follow me." We jumped up and walked by her into the store. She stopped in the middle of the room and said, "Well girls where shall we pitch our tent?" Rachel and Zada looked at each other and then at Aunt Blanche, and said "We don't know anything about a tent."

With a sly grin their aunt said, "We will all work to-gether, Rachel, move that stool out of the corner and Zada, help me with this table." In a little while the clothesline was stretched between a nail that held a big calendar on the wall and the top of a rack that held garden rakes. A saw horse was placed on each side of the rope and a bright colored quilt was draped over the line and rested on the sides of the saw horses.

Aunt Blanche stood back admiring their creation and said, "Girls, what do you think of your new place to sleep?" Rachel and Zada were so excited that they were jumping around and squealing. "Can we make our beds in the tent now, please Aunt Blanche?" "You sure can." Then in a more serious tone she said, "Try not to stay awake too long, because we strike camp at sun up." So the routine was set. Every evening after the store closed, camp was set up and each morning it was taken down before the store opened for business and the quilts and ropes were carried to the back rooms.

One morning after Aunt Blanche had been with the family for a week, Sairy asked the girls if they would like to go to Mrs. Parker's house to play. She said Joey could go along and play with Mrs. Parker's little boy. Mrs. Parker was a lady from the Methodist church that had taken Rachel and Zada to church occasionally.

Aunt Blanche made sure they were ready to go and after assuring Sairy that she would hurry back, they started the walk to the other side of town.

Mrs. Parker met them at the door and invited them in. She looked at Aunt Blanche, and said in a soft voice, "Is it time?" She answered with a nod of her head and then said. "You kids be good and mind Mrs. Parker." She left and Mrs. Parker soon had the three children seated around a table with picture books to look at.

When Aunt Blanche didn't come for them after supper, Mrs. Parker told them they were going to spend the night with her. They had never slept away from home before. She took them upstairs to a room that had a big bed for the girls and a cot for Joey. It was sure different from "camping."

After breakfast the next morning, they looked out the window and saw Aunt Blanche coming up the path. Rachel and Zada ran to meet her and Mrs. Parker invited her to come in and have coffee and a blackberry muffin. When they were seated at the table Aunt Blanche said, "Girls, I have some news, Dr. Goff came to the house last night and brought you a new baby brother."

Mrs. Parker smiled and said, "What did they name him?" "Ira Thomas, for both his grandpas," Aunt Blanche said.

Rachel was confused, but didn't say anything. Did the doctor bring him in his little black bag? She guessed she would have to wait until she got home to have her questions answered.

Aunt Blanche thanked Mrs. Parker and invited her to come and see the new baby. Rachel and Zada were anxious to get home but their aunt wouldn't let them run ahead. "You girls know Joey can't keep up with you, his legs are too short," she said, as she led the little boy along the road.

When they reached the store, Rachel walked slowly behind Aunt Blanche as they went thru the store to the back rooms. Her mom was in bed but looked up when they entered the room and said, "Girls, Joey, come see your new brother." Rachel edged up to the side of the bed and looked down at the small bundle wrapped in flannel that her mother was holding. It was the ugliest thing she had ever seen. It was red and wrinkled and didn't have any hair. It was hard for her to figure out why her mom had let Dr. Goff leave a baby like that. A kitten would have been much nicer to play with.

Their household revolved around the new baby. Zada and she soon learned they had to be quiet when Ira was sleeping. If they woke him, he might cry for hours. He had something that Aunt Blanche said was colic, and he would out grow it.

As they sat around the supper table, Rachel was sad when Aunt Blanche announced she would be going home tomorrow.

Sairy would miss having her to help with all the work around the house and care of the new baby.

The washing of clothes never seemed to be done. Water was carried from the well in the back yard and heated on the stove in the kitchen. The tubs and washboard were set up on a wooden bench and after the clothes were washed and rinsed the tubs were emptied and hung on a nail outside next to the back door. When the weather was warm and dry, the clothes were hung on lines outside and on rainy days a makeshift line was put up in one of the bedrooms.

Rachel and Zada were still "camping" in the store at night, but somehow it wasn't as exciting as it had been the first night.

Rachel was awakened one night by a strange unfamiliar sound. She sat up and looked around, thinking maybe some animal had gotten into the store. Zada started to cough and couldn't seem to stop. Then she paused and Rachel heard that sound again. The noise that had awakened her was not an animal sound but was coming from her sister.

Her heart began to pound and she could sense that Zada needed help. She threw her blanket to the side and ran to Aunt Blanche who was sleeping on a cot in the front room. As she shook her, she yelled, "Come quick, Zada is coughing and can't stop."

When Blanche reached Zada, she touched her head and knew she had a fever. She took her and laid her on the cot in the front room. She stirred up the fire in the cooking stove that had been banked for the night and pulled the teakettle to the hottest part of the stove.

When Sairy woke up, she wondered why Blanche and the girls were up this late at night. Maybe she was telling them stories, since she was going home tomorrow. She came out of the bedroom and immediately knew that something was wrong. When she saw Zada, and heard her cough, she turned to Blanche and said, "Do you think it is the croup?"

She didn't wait for her sister to answer but picked Zada up and sat down in the rocking chair and held her on her lap. "Rachel, bring me that brown bottle from the lower shelf." When Rachel handed her mother the bottle, she opened it and began to rub smelly stuff on Zada's neck and chest.

The tea kettle began to spit out little puffs of steam and soon a steady stream was coming from the kettle. Aunt Blanche grabbed a sheet from the cot and threw it over the back of the rocker, and extended it to the back of a kitchen chair. Sairy and Zada were enclosed in a makeshift tent and the steam from the teakettle was directed into it.

After a few minutes Zada coughed and spit up in the rag that Sairy held to her mouth. Rachel was standing beside the chair and her head began to swim as she saw some thick yellow stuff run down her sister's chin. Zada began to breathe easier and drifted off to sleep as her mother held her.

Blanche decided to stay a few more days until Zada was better. Two days later Joey started to cough and when Rachel complained of feeling hot the next day, Blanche said, "Sairy you better have Doc Goff drop by and check these youngin's." Sairy knew that Charlie wouldn't like to spend the three dollars Dr. Goff charged for a visit to the house, but her mind was made up,.That evening she sent word to Nell at the switchboard to get word to the doctor to stop by and see the kids.

Two days later at about dark Dr. Goff pulled up in front of the store in his buggy. He tied his horse to the hitching rail and walked up the steps and thru the store to the back rooms. Sairy was coughing occasionally and looked tired from the lack of sleep.

Dr. Goff surveyed the situation as he checked Sairy and the three kids. He studied how he should tell the family, when Blanche spoke up, "Is it the croup, Doc?" He looked from one of the women to the other before he said, "Ladies, I think we got us some cases of the whooping cough."

When Blanche told him about using the steam and camphorated oil, he said, "That's good. There is one other thing that will help. Take a cup of chopped onions and mix them with a couple tablespoons of butter and brown sugar, simmer the mixture on the back of the stove and give Zada a teaspoonful of the syrup when the coughing starts. This will help bring up the phlegm and prevent some of the choking. This disease is easy to spread. I'd say Zada and Rachel caught it at school. Several families have kids sick with bad coughs."

"Blanche, you and Charlie stay well and send word if you need me." Charlie had been standing in the doorway watching and when the doctor drove off in his buggy, he came back in and announced, "I'm shutting the store up and

134

going over to Dave's. I don't want to be catching this cough in my poor condition."

His brother lived up Yellow Creek about three miles from town. He and Dave liked to go coon hunting and this would be the perfect opportunity. He always complained of bad health and feeling poorly, but his condition always improved when he had a chance to go coon hunting or get in on a good fox chase.

Blanche was so angry it was hard to hold her tongue. She often wondered why her older sister had married him. It could've been to escape her home. Sairy had been kept home from school after she went part way through the fifth grade. She was needed at home to care for younger sisters and brothers.

At the age of sixteen when Charlie took a fancy to her, she jumped at the offer of marriage. She didn't know at the time that he was anxious to get a wife and get the farm and other things his father gave each of his children when they married.

After Charlie left Blanche looked at Sairy and said, "Don't worry Sis, we'll make out okay. The memories of the next few days were to haunt Blanche for the rest of her life.

Baby Ira began to cough the next day and Zada continued to have coughing spasms. Rachel and Joey coughed at night, but they didn't seem to be as sick as Zada. She stayed in bed and refused to eat. Sairy couldn't get her to drink anything except water and small amounts of weak tea.

Blanche never seemed to stop in her effort to care for the sick and keep the household running. She was well organized and the important things were getting done, until one evening she glanced across the room and saw Sairy in the rocking chair. Ira was fussing because the rocker had stopped and his mother was sound asleep. Blanche waited for Sairy to start rocking and when she didn't, she said, "Sairy, Ira is trying to talk to you; I think he likes it better when the chair is moving."

Sairy opened her eyes, but didn't answer and Ira began to cry louder. Blanche went to get the baby and when she was near the chair she could tell that something was wrong with her sister. Her faced was flushed and when she felt her forehead it was hot to touch. She helped Sairy to bed and laid Ira by her on the side of the bed that was pushed up against the wall.

Sairy was breathing hard and answered Blanche in a whisper when she tried to talk to her. For the first time since Dr. Goff had been there, Blanche was scared. She even forgot how mad she was at Charlie.

She needed help, but knew she couldn't leave the house. The situation seemed impossible until suddenly she had an idea. It was risky but she would have to take a chance. She sat down at the kitchen table and got out Zada's school tablet and pencil.

Rachel was the one in the family that felt the best, so Blanche decided to write a note and send it by Rachel to the house down the road. She didn't know the family's name but it was the only house in sight of the store. After the note was written, she explained to Rachel to knock on the door and give it to whoever answered and hurry back.

Blanche stood at the front door of the store and watched Rachel as she walked down the path. She tried to listen at the same time for any sounds from the back rooms. Rachel was soon back and told her aunt, "I gave the paper to the woman that came to the door, and came right back." Blanche told her she had done a good job and at the same time she felt guilty because Dr. Goff had left instructions that no one was to leave the house.

Something would have to be done about feeding little Ira, so Blanche decided to make gruel from oatmeal. She was able to get him to take a small amount, but he wasn't used to eating from a spoon and choked easily. She had seen her mother feed a baby kitten that the mother had abandon with a cloth soaked in milk. She tried it on Ira and it seemed to work a little better than the spoon.

Two days later, Della, Sairy's sister, came to help. Blanche had written in the note to try and get word to her dad and mom that Sairy and the kids were sick and she could use some help. She never mentioned that Charlie had left.

The neighbor's oldest boy was glad to take the message because his dad let him ride the mare that he had recently traded for.

When Della knocked at the store door, Blanche thought it was someone wondering why it was locked in the middle of the day. Several people had come and finally she decided to stop making excuses and simply said, "Charlie isn't here and I don't know when he will be back."

Rachel peeked out the door and saw her Aunt Della, "Aunt Blanche, Aunt Della is at the front door. Can I let her in?" Blanche ran past Rachel to the front door and with a big bear hug and smile she said, "Come on in Sis, I sure am glad to see you."

Della was puzzled at the store being closed. She looked around and said, "Where is Charlie?" Blanche rolled her eyes up to the ceiling and tried to keep her voice calm. "He's over at Dave's. I'll tell you about it later." "When dad got word you needed help, he told me to come ahead and he would try to find Dr. Goff and have him come by. Blanche told her that Dr. Goff had been there but Sairy and Ira weren't sick then.

Della jumped right in and did whatever she could and Blanche was able to get some short naps.

Dr. Goff had been out in the country delivering a baby and checking on a man that had a smashed leg from a timber accident. He came three days after Della had come to help and he didn't like what he found.

He was a soft-spoken man and everyone said there wasn't a mean bone in his body. "Where is Charlie?", He shouted so loud that Rachel ran and crouched behind the wicker rocker. After a quick check of everyone, He sat down at the kitchen table and asked Blanche and Della to pull up a chair and in a calmer voice, He said, "Girls, things are bad, Sairy has pneumonia and Zada's lungs are so weak that she probably won't pull out of it. Rachel and Joey will probably be all right with some rest, Give them all the water and juice they'll drink."

He was about to tell them about Ira when they heard Sairy try to scream. They all ran to the bed and Dr. Goff grabbed little Ira and pounded him on the back. Della began to cry, the baby was blue and she couldn't see his little chest moving. Dr. Goff put his finger in the baby's mouth and then held him by his feet over the bed. Next he breathed in his mouth and pushed on his chest. Blanche said in a trembling voice, "Doc, what do you want me to do?" "Nothing. He's gone. Your nephew was too weak to swallow and he choked to death."

Blanche was stunned but knew she had to keep going. She began to give orders. "Della, see to Zada. Rachel, play with Joey." Looking at Sairy she said, "Don't worry. He isn't suffering anymore.

When Dr. Goff was ready to leave, Blanche asked him if he could find Rev. Tom and tell him what happened. She didn't ask him to find Charlie; she only wanted to see the baby's grandfather. She didn't want to deal with the scum of the earth at this time.

Grey clouds were moving in the sky and threatened rain. The leaves on the trees swayed in the breeze, as a group of family members and neighbors were gathered around the mound of earth that lay beside the small grave that had been dug that morning for three week old Ira Thomas Bonnett.

Blanche had come to the service only because Sairy had pleaded with tears in her eyes, "Please Sis, I can't go and I want you to be with him to the end." Della and Mrs. Parker had stayed at the house with Sairy and the children.

Blanche had been brought up in a family that loved God and tried to do right by their neighbors, but she felt nothing but bitterness in her heart as she looked across the small casket at the father of the child.

When Reverend Tom had found his son and brought him home, he came into the house sobbing with his shoulders shaking and in a trembling voice, said, "My God, Why did you take my boy away? Why God?"

Blanche thought to herself, "Isn't that just like the creep, blaming God?" He probably knew it wouldn't be safe to blame anyone else. Pa thinks a lynch mob would be too good for him.

Reverend Tom had taken charge and made all the arrangements. He didn't say what he said to Charlie, when he had found Dave and him sitting on the creek bank fishing, except that they had a long talk.

This had been a difficult service for Reverend Tom to conduct. He cherished his grandchildren and had looked forward to the time that Ira would be big enough to run to meet him when he came to visit. He had spent a lot of time talking to God since Dr. Goff had told him about his son's family. He prayed that God would watch over the sick and that he would be forgiven for failing to teach his son to take responsibility for his family.

When Reverend Tom had talked with his wife Ruth and told her how he felt, she had looked at him in disgust. Ruth supported her husband in his church work and was a loving wife, but she was known far and wide for her quick temper and sometimes speaking her mind before thinking of what the results might be.

"Tom Bonnett, you listen to me. It isn't anything we did or didn't do to make Charlie act like he does. If it was our fault, the other four kids would have turned out rotten to the core. We can't say that one bad apple spoils the whole barrel."

Tom looked at his wife with a slight smile, and said, "Can't we even pray for our son to change?" "Oh, I'll do that all right, but I'm not going to add to God's work by asking him to forgive me for something I didn't do."

All these thoughts kept running thru Tom's head as he read the scriptures and lead the group in Sairy's favorite hymn, *Amazing Grace*. A few drops of rain had begun to fall as he looked up with outstretched arms and said, "Heavenly Father, I commit this child to your tender care." He then looked around the group and as his gaze rested on his son, he said, "The Lord bless and keep you, the Lord watch over you now and for evermore." As was his custom at the end of any service, he moved his arms as if he were gathering the group together and said, "Go in peace. Amen."

Rachel and Joey had been sent to the back yard to play, but Joey wasn't interested in the pictures that his sister was drawing with a stick in the bare spot on the ground where the wash water had been emptied. He toddled back to the house in search of one of Aunt Blanche's buttermilk cookies and his favorite blanket.

Rachel had been told that Grandpa Tom was going to the church to have a funeral for baby Ira and that she was to be a big girl and help take care of Joey while Aunt Blanche was gone. She couldn't understand why she was needed with Della, Mrs. Parker, Zada and her mom in the house. Lately Zada didn't say much and didn't want to play with her. Her mom sat in the rocker and sang while she held her and other times she cried softly and looked at the bed where Ira had slept.

As Rachel sat in the back yard, she wondered what "a funeral" meant. Suddenly she thought, "Why can't I go to the church and watch? I remember when Mrs. Parker took me to Sunday School. It isn't very far. Joey doesn't want to play, and no one will know that I am gone. I'll hurry back."

The cemetery was at the side of the church not more than a half mile from the Bonnett house. Rachel's curiosity increased as she made her way to the church. She heard singing as she came in sight of the church. She slipped in back of the building and peeped around the corner. A bunch of people were standing around a hole in the ground and Granddad Tom was talking to them. She saw her dad standing beside Grandma Ruth with a sad look on his face. Maybe he was sorry that baby Ira had gone to live with Jesus in heaven while he was at Uncle Dave's house fishing. Maybe he had wanted to tell him good-bye before he left.

Rachel thought Aunt Blanche looked different; she wasn't smiling like she did most of the time. She just stared at the little box that had been made for Ira to sleep in on his way to God's house.

After watching and listening for a while, Rachel decided that she had better go home before Joey missed her. She was just coming over the bank when she saw him come out the back door. He had come out outside looking for Rachel after tiring of watching the big people in the house. No one wanted to play or do any of the fun things like Aunt Blanche did.

Rachel thought about telling Joey how she had sneaked to the church and watched the grownups, but decided not to. What would a little kid like him understand anyway? He might tell Mommy that she had left the yard. Besides she couldn't explain it to Joey when she didn't understand what it was all about. It must be one of those things that Aunt Blanche says, "Don't worry; you'll understand it when you get older."

Two days after the funeral Charlie reopened the store and vowed he was going to do better by Sairy and the kids. Zada coughed less and she seemed to be a little better each day. Sairy thought, "If I can get her through the winter, she'll be better when spring comes."

Before Blanche and Della went home the following weekend, they cleaned the house, did the washing and baked a batch of bread and cookies. Sairy was sorry to see her sisters go but knew her mom needed them at home. She was expecting a new baby next month Rachel and Joey were about the same age as Sairy's brother Zeb and sister Emmie.

Rachel and Joey liked to walk thru the store on their way to the front yard and gaze at the peppermint sticks and chocolate drops that were on the counter in big glass jars. Their dad had a standard answer when they asked for a piece of candy. "No, it will stunt your growth."

Rachel had asked her Aunt Blanche what "stunt" meant the first time her dad told her that. Her aunt tried to explain what the word meant but all she could remember was that it had something to do with being little.

Rachel wondered why all the kids that came to the store and were given candy by their parents didn't look any different from her or Joey. One day she decided to find out. While her dad was helping Widow Jones load her groceries in the back of her wagon, she motioned for Joey to be quiet as she ran behind the counter and took the lid off the jar of peppermint sticks. She grabbed four sticks and shoved them down in her dress pocket and ran into the front room and out the kitchen door Joey was right behind her and they didn't stop until they were at the side of the house under the lilac bush.

"Joey, are you sure you want to eat this candy? You might shrivel up and be no bigger than our old tom cat." Joey thought his sister was josin' him and he thought about what he had heard his dad say, but the smell and sight of those sticks with the red strips winding around them were more than he could resist. "Rachel, you eat one first and I'll watch and see if you get little." Rachel looked at her brother and said, "I snitched them so it's only fair that you go first." "Oh all right, but if I get as little as that old cat it will be your fault."

Rachel thought a while and didn't like the idea of something happening to her brother. She remembered Ira and the whooping cough that the entire family had recently and she had another plan. We'll start eating at the same time and if we both shrink maybe no one will notice. They sat there and savored every lick of the sticks until they heard their mother call, then they shoved what was left in their mouths and begin to chew as fast as they could .Rachel said, "We're at the side of the house building a road with rocks and moss." She knew she wasn't supposed to tell things that weren't true, but this was different. She needed time to see if her brother was going to shrink.

Joey and Rachel stared at each other waiting for something to happen. They weren't sure what was supposed to happen. Maybe their fingers would get shorter first so they fixed their gaze on their hands and were very quiet. After waiting for what seemed like forever, Joey began to squirm and Rachel decided they had better go back in the house and see what their mother wanted. Rachel wiped Joey's face with the tail of her skirt and said, "Come on Joey, I don't think anything is going to happen." He jumped up with a big smile on his face and said, "Oh goody we can get some more candy again." "No Joey, that would be stealing. Today we were just eating the candy to see what would happen to us. Since we know that candy don't make you get little, we won't get anymore candy until Aunt Blanche comes at Christmas."

Rachel and Joey missed their aunt, no one seemed to laugh or talk to them since she had to go home to help Grandma Clara. Rachel learned two important things that day, first candy doesn't make you shrink and second, her dad didn't always tell the truth.

After tending the store for a while, Charlie began to become restless and found excuses for closing early and sometimes leaving for two or three days to go to his brother Dave's house. They fished and loafed around while Sairy was left home with the three kids and the store to run. She had to keep the store open because it was now also the post office.

Charlie announced one day when he came home from Dave's that he wanted to move to Wadesville. Sairy looked at him in disbelief and wondered what the family would do in a big town like that. She didn't say anything but waited for him to continue. "A traveling salesman was at the auction that Hosey Clarkson had Saturday. He told Dave and me the farm tool factory was hiring and he was sure that we could find work if we didn't mind leaving the hill country."

Dave wasn't interested in leaving the security of the farm that his dad had given him but Charley began to dream of life in a town and not being tied down to a store. He would be free after a shift in the factory to do whatever he fancied. He forgot that he had had similar feelings when he was on the farm. The store was to be a place to sit around and spin tales with his friends while Sairy did most of the work. She wouldn't have any problem watching the three kids since they would live in the back part of the building. He could forget all about caring for animals and hoeing corn and he would become a gentleman store proprietor.

These dreams were shattered when Sairy had a new baby and the kids got sick. He would never forget the way his parents had talked to him when the boy died. He had to admit to himself that the store hadn't been such a good idea after all.

He didn't ask Sairy if she would like to move, instead he said, "I'm getting a ride to Wadesville in two weeks when the salesman comes thru again."

Charley had a way of talking that made people like him when they first met, so it was no surprise when he came back and said, "I've got a job and will start to work as soon as we get moved." The foreman promised that he would find him a house and for him to go back and get his family.

Sairy had adjusted to life in the back of the store and wondered how her life would change in the days ahead.

She didn't question her husband's decision, but said, "when do you reckin' we'll be leaving?" Charlie looked at Sairy with a determined look and said, "the sooner the better." He got up and went behind the counter and tore a piece of butcher paper from the roll and wrote on it in big letters, *STORE FOR SALE*. He took it and propped it up on a box in the front window. As he came back he said to Sairy, "You best be getting things together." He had no doubt that someone would want the store right away.

Word got around and in less than a month a man had bought the store for a bargain. Some said that Charlie sold the store for a song and sang it himself.

They had enough money to pay Dave to move them in his Model-A Ford truck that he had recently bought to use on the farm. As Rachel, Zada and Joey piled in back of the truck, Rachel wondered if they would fall out. It made a loud noise and their mom told them to sit down and not to get up until they reached their new home and they would be all right. All three of them sat on a mattress and leaned their backs against a dish cupboard. Dave and Charlie tied a rope around the furniture and after they cranked the engine the truck started and they took off down the road.

Rachel had seen a few cars when people had driven them to the store, but most people still had horses and wagons. She was scared at first but soon began to enjoy listening to the rattle of the truck and the wind blowing in her face and her hair flying in all directions. Zada and Joey were more afraid. Zada's knuckles were white as she gripped the side of the truck. Joey's eyes got big as a tear trickled down his cheek. Some of their fear seemed to go away as they looked at Rachel and saw what a great time she was having.

It was supper time when the truck stopped in front of a small grey house that sat back from the brick street. Rachel got down from the truck and looked around and the first thing she saw after the house was the biggest building she had ever seen. It was tall, made of bricks and had windows all around it. She was still staring when a lady walked up and said, "I'm Donnie from down the street and when I saw the truck, I thought I'd come by and welcome you to the neighborhood." Sairy shook hands and said, "I'm Sairy and I'm glad to make your acquaintance."

Donnie looked at Rachel, who was still looking at the big building and said, "I hope you like your new school." It was the most fascinating thing that Rachel had ever seen. It was nothing like the one room school that she had started to when they lived on the farm or the two room one she had gone to recently.

As Rachel looked, she decided that the school playground was two times as big as the one at her old school. She thought how much fun it would be to try and throw a rock at the red brick wall and miss the windows. She kept these thoughts to herself as she began to help carry things into their new house.

Charlie started his new job at the factory and seemed content. He liked to sit around at lunch time and tell the other men of the great store that he had before coming to work at the factory. He told them he would have still been at the store, but his wife didn't like living in the country and wanted to move to town. The men thought he must be a good man to give up a fine store and move to town just to please his wife.

Their opinion changed when one of the wives went to visit Sairy and heard her talking about living in the back of the store and how surprised she had been when she heard they were moving and Charlie had a job in the factory.

The workers figured out that the store wasn't nearly as big as he described it and they shouldn't believe every thing he told them.

Sairy hadn't had to worry about knowing where her kids were before moving to town. Now they seemed to run around the neighborhood and didn't always answer when she called.

Charlie started staying late after work and playing cards with some of the men. Sairy didn't know they were playing poker and gambling for money until one day Charlie didn't have the rent money when the landlord came to collect.

He told Sairy that he was just trying to forget the boring job of fitting handles on shovels all day and hadn't noticed how much money he had lost in the game. Sairy knew that his father, Tom would be hurt if he knew his son was gambling and his mother, Ruth, would give him a tongue lashing like no son had ever heard. She was glad they didn't live near them.

The landlord gave them until the end of the week to raise the money. Sairy knew that something had to be done or her kids would be without a roof over their heads.

She and Donnie had become good friends and she went down the street to talk with her. When she heard of Sairy's troubles, she said, "Maybe I can help you find some work. What can you do?" Sairy said, "I'll try anything, but I've never done anything much except take care of the kids and house, "Donnie said," You drop by tomorrow and I'll let you know if I've found anything."

The next evening when Sairy knocked on the door, Donnie was all smiles. "Come in and have a cup of coffee, while I tell you the good news. One family needs their washing done because they have a new baby and the mother can't lift the tubs of water yet. Also the preacher's wife said she had been looking for someone to clean the windows and scrub the floors. She said her rheumatism had been acting up and she would be glad to have some help." This was the beginning of Sairy's career as a cleaning woman.

Rachel began wandering around the neighborhood and Joey was usually with her, because most of the time there was no one at home. Their mother had built up a cleaning business and had a different house to go to each day of the week.

Zada was a big girl of 13 and had a job washing dishes in a family restaurant after school and weekends. She worked hard and earned a little money and was assured of one good meal every day.

Charlie had been let go from the factory for frequently being late for work and not meeting the quota of attaching shovel handles during a shift. The day he was fired from his job he told Sairy that, "the boss picks on me and the job is boring." He didn't look for work, but was content to stay around the house and read "Wild West" books one of the families Sairy worked for had given her. He had a weekly poker game he went to and sometimes they played at his house.

Sairy had been bothered with "weak knees" since early childhood. Her mom said it was growing pains and she would outgrow it. At times the problem did seem to go away, but it still flared up from time to time. Recently Sairy's knees had been aching and it was harder each day to clean the floors in the houses where she worked. Most of the women that she worked for felt like the floors weren't clean and just didn't look right unless she scrubbed them with a brush and rag while crawling around on her hands and knees.

One morning Sairy awoke after a restless night and as she tried to sit up on the side of the bed she cried out as a sharp pain hit her in the lower part of her back. She fell back on the pillow and began to gasp in fast short breaths. She was determined not to cry out again. The pain had let up some, but she discovered that she could not bend her knees. They were stiff and felt hot when she laid her hands on them.

Charlie hadn't come home last night, which often happened when the group got together to play poker.

Zada had heard her mother and came to see what the noise was. When Sairy saw her daughter, she said, "Zada, wake up Rachel and Joey and tell them to get ready for school and then go down the street and ask Donnie if she'll get word to the Anderson family that I won't be there today."

When Zada came back from Donnie's, Sairy was still in bed. She looked at the drawn expression on her mother's face and said, "Mom, do you want me to stay home with you?" "No Sissy, you go on to school. I'll be all right until you come back for lunch. Make sure Rachel and Joey eat something before they leave and that they comb their hair." Combing his hair was something Joey didn't like to do and Rachel was usually too busy to bother with hers unless her mother reminded her.

When Charlie came home, he found his wife still in bed with a glass of water on a chair beside her. He had failed to see the biscuits and gravy on the back of the stove that he usually found that Sairy would leave for him before going to work. He was tired and sleepy and in no mood to see Sairy neglecting the cooking by lying around in bed. "Woman, I want my breakfast, what's the matter with you?" Sairy tried to explain that her back hurt and her knees wouldn't bend right. He shrugged his shoulders and said, "If I can't get anything to eat here, I'll go some place where I can." The tears trickled down her face as she heard the front door slam. Sairy realized that her husband was following his pattern of turning away from unpleasant situations. She never knew if or when she would see him again.

Rachel and Joey ran across the school yard when the bell rang to dismiss for lunch. They were surprised to see their mother still in bed. The only time that Rachel could remember her mother staying in bed this long was when everyone was sick and Ira had died. Fear gripped her as she wondered what they would do without Aunt Blanche.

Zada found some leftover cornbread and beans from yesterday's supper for their lunch and promised her mother that she would come home after school before she went to her job at the restaurant.

Rachel went back to school but she didn't hear much of the history lesson, and the fractions all seemed to jumble like chunks of vegetables in a pot of stew. She tried to pay attention but her mind kept wandering back to her mother lying in bed. What would they do?

Later that afternoon Sairy heard someone knock on the door and then she heard Donnie call out, "Sairy, are you in there?" "In here Donnie, come on in." Donnie made her way to the bedroom and said, "What happened to you? I've never seen you in bed at this hour of the day?"

Sairy told her friend how she felt and about Charlie leaving. Donnie knew that Charlie was not a devoted husband and didn't provide well for his family but she didn't think anyone would walk out when someone was sick. Sairy had not confided in her friend about Charlie's behavior when the family had whooping cough and Ira had died. She had simply said that she had a son that died from a bad cough.

Sairy was in bed 10 days before she was able to get up and walk about the house. Zada, Rachel and Joey went to school and Zada was sometimes able to bring food home from the restaurant after work. The owner of the restaurant suspected that there was trouble at home and he would say things like "Zada, take this stew home, nobody will buy it tomorrow." There always seemed to be something left over at the end of the day for her to take home. Sairy was thankful for the food that Zada was able to bring home but she didn't know what to think when Rachel and Joey brought in celery, lettuce and cabbage one evening. Sairy dreaded the thought that her children were hungry enough to steal. She wondered what to say to them. They seemed so pleased with themselves. They had come into the house and put the vegetables on the table and said, "Look what we got mom." Sairy looked at her children and with a stern voice said, "Where did you get this stuff?" Rachel suddenly realized that her mother thought they had stolen the vegetables. "We didn't steal anything, honest Mom."

Joey spoke up, "Katherine and Dennis Snyder asked us if we wanted to go with them to get vegetables." Rachel continued, "They live under the railroad bridge in a grey house and have lots of brothers and sisters. They all have to work and Katherine and Dennis's job is to go to the train station and check the garbage cans when the train stops and the old vegetables are thrown out of the refrigerator cars. Sometimes the vegetables aren't very good, but they always get something."

Sairy's chest felt tight and she swallowed back the lump in her throat as she eyed the wilted lettuce and limp celery stalks on the table. "They'll do just fine. Zada gets paid today and we'll buy some potatoes to cook with the cabbage and celery and we'll have a feast."

Sairy knew she had to go back to work and wondered how she would be able to scrub floors as she had before.

One day when the preacher had come to visit, he didn't ask about Charlie. He hadn't seen him around and the whole neighborhood knew the family situation but didn't ask questions when they talked to Sairy. Reverend Bailey looked at Sairy and said. "My wife would sure miss you coming to clean every Thursday but I heard of a job that you might like better. The children's home on the other side of town is looking for a cook. I can take you to see about it in a couple of days if you think you might be interested. I can't go tomorrow because I have a wedding to perform. You think it over and send one of the kids to let me know what you decide."

That evening when Zada came home from work, Sairy gathered her kids around the kitchen table and told them of her decision. "Zada, Rachel and Joey, I've thought a lot about the job at the children's home that Reverend Bailey told me about, and I think I have to look into it. It would mean that I wouldn't be close the school and you would be on your own until I came home at night. You would need to get your own lunch or take it with you every morning. What do you all think?"

Joey's head had dropped and he starred at the floor. He knew that big boys didn't cry and if you did the bigger kids called you a sissy or a Mama's baby. He would miss his mom not being there when he ran across the playground and in the front door at the close of school each day. Zada said, "I'll get home as soon as I can after work and I'll check on things at lunch time." Rachel with a mischievous grin on her face said, "Ah shucks mom, Joey and I will be just fine."

Sairy said, "I might not get the job but I have to try. We need the money. Zada, will you stop at the Bailey's on your way to work tomorrow and tell Reverend Bailey that I would like to know more about the cooking job."

Three days later Sairy and Reverend Bailey stopped in front of a big two story brick building. Sairy's heart raced and her hands were sweaty as she sat across from the superintendent of the home and answered questions. She had never applied for a job and she didn't know what to expect. Mr. Edgell was impressed with Sairy's straightforward answers and her eagerness to work, and she got the job.

The family adjusted to Sairy leaving the house every morning at 5:30 a.m., except Sunday, and coming home at 6:30 in the evening. Sairy was glad she could ride the street car most of the way to work. She enjoyed her job but felt sorry for the children who were in the home because they didn't have anyone to care for them.

She knew her kids didn't see much of her, but with the money she was bringing home every Friday on pay day, she was able to pay the rent and buy groceries. This was the first time that she had had money to manage, but Sairy was a quick learner and she felt a sense of pride when she realized that there would soon be enough money to buy new shoes for Joey.

She kept the money in an empty tin baking powder can on the shelf of the cupboard behind the milk pitcher. Every Sunday afternoon, Sairy and the kids sat around the table and counted the money in the can.

It was Saturday morning after Sairy and Zada had left for work that Rachel and Joey looked up from their marble game and saw their dad coming up the walk of the school. The neighborhood kids gathered at the school yard to play marbles and other games every Saturday. None of the other kids had arrived yet. As Charlie approached them, he said,

"You kids run in the house and get your clothes, you're going for a ride with me." They jumped up and ran across the playground and into the house and grabbed their sweaters off the nail behind the door. This was exciting. They didn't know their dad had a car. Their mother hadn't told them where their dad was or why he had left.

Rachel had wondered but had never asked. Maybe he had been working and had bought a car. When they came up to the car their dad said, "You kids climb in the rumble seat." They were surprised to see a woman in the front seat of the car. She stared straight ahead and said, "I hope you know what you're doing. You are going to get us both in trouble."

Rachel and Joey thought their dad wanted to show off the new car by taking them a ride around the neighborhood. They didn't know what to think when they turned onto a busy road.

The air was hot and black clouds gathered in the sky. Rachel and Joey felt the first drops of rain and then it began to rain hard. They crouched down in the seat and pulled their sweaters over their heads. They were soaked when the car stopped and their dad said, "Get out and run to the porch."

Rachel saw a small grey house with a porch that extended a short distance on each side of the front door. Two stove pipes protruded from the roof but Rachel didn't see any smoke from either one. The woman was right behind them as they stepped up on the porch. She looked at Charlie and said, "So this is Rachel and Joey. I can't see how they'll be much help." Charlie said, "Now Thelma, they'll surprise you. They know how to do a lot of things. Rachel can even cook some."

At least they knew the woman's name and Rachel got the idea that this was more than a visit with their dad. He looked at them and said, "Thelma has been feeling poorly

and you kids can help with some of the work around here."
Joey looked at Rachel and began to cry, "I want to go home. I
want my mommy."

They settled into a routine of carrying in wood for the
cook stove, washing dishes, feeding the chickens and
whatever else their dad or Thelma wanted them to do.
Thelma spent most of her time sewing pieces of rags into
long strips that she said would make a nice rug when she had
enough.

Rachel had guessed that although there were no
houses in sight that there was a town nearby. Their dad went
to the store almost every day to talk with the other men that
gathered on the porch of the store. Thelma had come up with
a change of clothes for Rachel and Joey from the bag of
things that she collected from the neighbors for her rugs.

Rachel missed her mom and Joey cried until he fell
asleep at night. One day when they were in the chicken house
gathering eggs, she thought to herself, "Why can't we fly
away like a chicken? Well maybe not a chicken, because they
don't go any farther than from a low tree branch to the
ground." If she could fly like a sparrow, she could get back
home to Zada and her mother.

They had been with their father almost two weeks
and Rachel knew she didn't want to stay any longer. She had
an idea. She would run away and take Joey with her. That
night after she was sure her dad and Thelma were asleep, she
crept to the other side of the room where Joey lay sleeping on
a quilt on the floor. They each had a bed made on the front
room floor. Rachel motioned for Joey to be still and to
follow her. She had taken their other set of clothes, two
biscuits and two apples and hid them under a bush in the
yard. They walked all night on the road, not knowing where
they were going.

At daybreak Rachel decided to ask the first person they saw if they were on the road to Wadesville. As they continued to walk, they heard a wagon approaching. A man with a load of hay pulled up beside them. Rachel was afraid at first that the man might take them back to their dad. She had to think fast. "Mornin', you kids are out early, where you headed?" "Wadesville," Rachel answered with her best grown up voice. The man looked up and down the road and said, "You're headed in the wrong direction." Rachel said, "We're looking for our grandfather. Do you know where Ira Reed lives?" "Sure Ira and Clara live about 10 miles from here on the old Martin place. If you want a ride, hop on the back of the wagon. I'm going part way."

They sat on the back of the wagon with their legs hanging over the edge and they leaned back against the hay. Rachel decided that it was time for breakfast, so they each ate a biscuit as they bounced along the road. The wagon stopped at a fork in the road and the farmer said, "Well kids you should be able to find your way. Your grandpa lives three or four miles down the road." Rachel thanked him for the ride and they started to walk again.

The sun was going down when Rachel and Joey saw their grandpa's house. As they walked up the path Grandma Clara opened the front door and said, "Ira, come here. Sairy's kids Rachel and Joey are here." Rachel explained to her grandparents that they had run away from their dad and was trying to get back to their mom. They said Thelma wasn't mean to them but they had to wait on her all the time and do most of the work.

The next few days were busy for Rachel and Joey. Their grandparents made sure they helped Zeb and Emmie with the chores. They were the youngest children of Ira and Clara and near the age of Rachel and Joey. Zeb was the oldest of the four and delighted in bossing the other three kids around.

One day Emmie found a dead baby chicken in the coop and Zeb announced, "You kids come with me; we're having a funeral." They followed him out behind the barn and he said."Emmie, you go in the house and get a shoe box and a rag. Rachel and Joey, start digging the grave with this hoe." Emmie said to Zeb, "What are you going to do if we do all the work?" "I'm the preacher and I'll preach the sermon" answered Zeb. The three of them looked at each other and Rachel said, "That ain't fair." Zeb didn't want anything to ruin the chicken's funeral, so he said, "Well all right. Emmie, you can sing, Rachel, you can pray, and Joey, you can put the casket in the ground, and we'll all cover it with dirt. That seemed fair and they all agreed to do as Zeb planned.

Rachel and Joey started to dig and Emmie was soon back with the box and a rag. She wrapped the chicken in a piece of grandma's old blue apron and when Rachel and Joey had dug the hole to please Zeb, the service began.

Zeb talked and Emmie sang *Jesus Loves Me.* Rachel prayed and tried to sound like Grandpa Tom. "God, watch over this little chicken until its mamma gets there to help you. Thank you for not letting Emmie get caught when she swiped the box and the rag. AMEN.

" Zeb said, "To make sure the chicken goes to heaven there is one more thing we need to do." He reached in his overall pocket and pulled out a round shinny box. He raised his voice and said, "Sisters and brothers, step forward and get a rub of snuff." Zeb put some in his mouth and handed the box to Rachel. She said, "I don't want any of this stuff. It looks dirty." Zeb replied, "If anyone at the funeral refuses to put some snuff in their mouth, the chicken will go straight to hell." Rachel and Joey didn't know what hell was but figured it must be something really bad. Grandpa Tom had talked one time in church about hell, but all Rachel could remember was that it was a bad place.

None of the three wanted anything else bad to happen to the chick. The big calico cat had already choked it until it died. Rachel took a step toward Zeb and he handed her the snuff box. She tilted the can and some of the bitter brown powder fell into her mouth. Emmie and Joey did the same and handed the can back to Zeb. Rachel had never tasted anything so awful in her life but she was afraid to spit it out. Zeb might say she had to do it again, so she decided to swallow it and save the chicken. Emmie and Joey began immediately to slobber and spit and Zeb laughed until he cried at the sight. They weren't thinking of the chicken, all they wanted to do was get rid of the vile tasting stuff. The funeral was over when Zeb said, "God bless you all for coming."

They went back to the wood yard and began to carry wood into the house to fill the kindling box. Rachel's head began to spin as she bent over to pick up a piece of wood. Hot water ran from her nose and mouth and she had never felt so terrible in all her life. She fell to the ground and began to vomit.

Zeb was feeling guilty and a little scared. He thought anyone would have better sense than to swallow snuff. He ran to the kitchen to get his mother. As Joey saw Grandma Clara running, he wondered if his sister was going to die like Baby Ira had. She knelt beside Rachel and took one look at the brown stuff on the ground and suspected what had happened. She had one way to prove it and said to Rachel, "You're getting to be a big girl now. Would you like some of grandma's snuff?" She pulled her snuff box from her pocket and Rachel began to wretch and vomit again at the sight of the box. Zeb said, "Want me to help her in the house?" "No, just bring the cushion from the chair in the front room and put her head on it. I'll go fix her some medicine."

Clara wasn't gone long until she came back carrying a glass of pale yellow liquid. With a sharp voice she said, "Sit up Rachel and drink all of this." Rachel could tell that her grandma was in no mood to be asked questions. So she sat up and drank the liquid. It tasted awful but it couldn't compare to the snuff she had swallowed. She made a face and her grandma said, "Straighten up, a little mustard water never hurt anyone." Almost immediately Rachel realized what her grandma was trying to do. She wanted to wash the snuff out of her stomach. Her medicine worked because Rachel began to vomit again.

She knew that she was going to die and she wished her mom and Grandpa Tom were there. Emmie saw why her mother didn't want Rachel in the house. The mess was bad enough in the wood yard. Rachel said to herself, "God get me through this and I'll never touch tobacco as long as I live."

Clara was a woman of few words and folks said you could tell what she was thinking by the sparks coming from her copper colored hair. Zeb wasn't surprised when she looked at him and said, "Your pa will take care of you when he comes in from the hay field."

She turned to go into the house as if nothing had happened and said, "You youngin's get to weedin' the garden." She took the cushion with her and Rachel knew she was expected to do her part of the garden work.

Rachel didn't like staying with her grandma and grandpa, but it was better than staying with her dad and waiting on Thelma all day long. Zeb and Emmie talked mean to them and tried to make her and Joey do most of the chores. She spent a lot of time day dreaming about what her

160

and Joey should do as she pulled weeds from around the carrots.

When Zada had come home that evening, she didn't see Rachel and Joey. She was tired and didn't feel like hunting them. They knew they weren't supposed to leave the house but sometimes they wondered around the neighborhood. She wanted to find them before her mother came home. She didn't need anything else to worry about. She had a lot on her mind adjusting to the new job and her dad moving out.

She walked up and down the street and circled the block behind the school but no one had seen them. She decided to fix supper while she waited for her mom to come home, maybe they would show up. An hour later she heard her mom on the porch and as she opened the door she called out, "Hi kids." When she looked at Zada, she knew something was wrong. Zada looked up from the skillet of potatoes that she was stirring and said, "I don't know where Rachel and Joey are. I looked around the neighborhood, but no one has seen them." It was supper time and they always came home when they got hungry.

Sairy decided she had to do something, it was getting dark. She told Zada to stay at the house in case they came home. She was going to Donnie's house to call Reverend Bailey to see what he thought she should do.

The preacher and his wife came to the house about nine o'clock expecting to see Rachel and Joey safe and sound. When he saw the worried look on Sairy and Zada's faces, he knew the children were still missing. He laid his hand on Sairy's shoulder and said, "Sairy I think we should let the sheriff know about this." Sairy nodded her head in agreement. She felt like she would burst into tears if she tried to talk. He looked at his wife and said, "Lottie, you stay with Sairy while I go make the call."

He came back in a little while and said, "The sheriff will check it out and he said to let him know if they come home."

Three weeks had past and Rachel and Joey were still gone. Sairy continued to work during the day and cry at night. Donnie had promised Sairy that if they came home she would keep an eye on them until she or Zada got in from work.

After getting home from the post office, Zada propped up the envelope in front of the sugar bowl on the table. It didn't look like a bill. The writing was bold and uneven on the envelope. Her mother would tell her about it when she came home. Lately she had talked with her more than usual. Zada knew she was worried and lonely. Her mother read the letter as soon as she came home and then handed it to Zada. It simply said. "Sairy, your kids are here. Come and get them, Pa. Zada remembered her grandad as a man of few words, who seldom smiled. Sairy had mixed emotions. She was glad because Rachel and Joey were alive, but disgusted because her dad hadn't given her any details.

Sairy sent Zada up the street to give Donnie the good news and to ask her to call Reverend Bailey. The preacher came early the next morning to see what he could do to help. After he and Sairy talk they decided they needed someone with a car to take Sairy to get Rachel and Joey.

Donnie had come soon after Reverend Bailey and said maybe her husband could go if they didn't mind riding in the rumble seat of their little car. The preacher saw the worried look on Sairy's face and knew she didn't have money to pay for the gasoline. Sairy, the church wants to help so we will buy the gas for Luke's car.

That evening Sairy got out of the car in front of the house where she had spent the first 16 years of her life. Thinking back she realized that she had thought that getting married would help her to have a better life. A life where she didn't have to take care of younger brothers and sisters and help with everything her mother couldn't get done with a new baby coming every two years or sooner. In a way she was worse off because her dad provided for his family and her husband didn't like to work and always complained of "feeling poorly." When Rachel and Joey saw the car and saw their mother get out they ran down the bank from the garden and flung themselves into her arms. They both began to talk at the same time and in a short while they had told every detail of the past three weeks except Rachel being sick at the chicken funeral.

Ira seemed to delight in telling Sairy what a no good skunk she had married and today was no exception. Sairy hated for her dad to talk like this while Luke stood by and pretended not to hear. He kept making small talk with the kids until finally he said, "Sairy we best get started back before dark."

After Sairy had thanked her Ma and Pa and the kids had climbed in the rumble seat, they were on their way home.

She didn't know where Charlie was and she hadn't told anyone that she had another baby on the way. She thought he suspected, because he had left soon after he had heard her vomiting one morning.

Just last week one of the young kitchen helpers at the children's home had lost her job because she was pregnant. The superintendent had said, "We can't have people working

here in the 'family way', the children might ask questions."
Sairy knew she wouldn't have a job much longer, but she
tried not to think about it, right now she was just glad to have
Rachel and Joey back.

Sairy lost her job sooner than she thought she would.
The next week she became dizzy and fainted while she was
stirring a big pot of soup. The kitchen was very hot and she
told the supervisor that she got over heated. Two days later
she became dizzy again. This time the supervisor simply
said, "Sairy you can finish out the week and then we can't use
you anymore. You know our rule about women in the family
way. We can't have the children asking questions."

Sairy went home that night with a heavy heart. She
had been able to manage up until now, but she didn't see
anyway out of their problems. She had a talk with Donnie
and they decided that she might get some of her old cleaning
jobs back that she had before she started to work at the
children's home. She hoped this would give her time to think
of some way to care for her kids and the new baby that was
coming.

Sairy did get some of her cleaning jobs back but the
pay wasn't enough to keep the house. With the help of the
church she moved the four of them to a third floor flat. It
wasn't as big as the house and Rachel and Joey missed the
schoolyard and playing with their friends. Zada continued her
job in the restaurant and her younger brother and sister began
to sell newspapers on the street.

Sairy knew that the pain in her back was not to be
ignored when it came around to the bottom of her belly. Her
back often ached when she came in from cleaning at the end
of the day, but this feeling was different. It would stop and
then start again in a little while. She remembered the four
other times when labor had started, but she hadn't had the

feeling of desperation that was coming over her now. Her sister Blanche had been with her and knew what to do and how to make everyone stay calm.

Zada was coming up the stairs when she heard a slight moan. She ran into the room at the top of the stairs and saw her mother leaning against the kitchen table. Her fists were clinched and beads of sweat stood out on her forehead. She had heard about labor pains but this baby wasn't supposed to come for two weeks. Her mother said, "Sissy, go down stairs and see if Mrs. Lucas is home. Tell her I would like to see her if she isn't busy." Zada turned without saying a word and darted down the steps to the first floor and began to knock on the landlady's door.

When she opened the door and saw Zada, she knew that this call was more than a tenant that had come to complain about something. "What's wrong Zada? You look as white as a sheet." Zada said, "Mom want's you to come up if you are not too busy." "I guess I could set the skillet of potatoes off the fire that I was frying for supper and come up for a minute." Mrs. Lucas knew when a renter had a problem that the best thing to do was check it out or they pestered you until something was done.

Sairy hadn't asked for anything before so maybe whatever she wanted could wait until tomorrow. She looked at Zada and thought to herself, no wonder the girl is pale she works too hard in that restaurant. Mrs. Lucas followed Zada up the stairs and when she opened the door she was shocked to see Sairy sitting at the kitchen table with pool of water on the floor around her feet. She had given birth to four sons and two daughters. That had been a long time ago and she had grandchildren now, but she could remember what it felt like before they made their way into the world.

She motioned with her hand and said, "Zada, help me get your mom to the bedroom, and then go ask John to see if he can find Doc Adams and bring him here. Then sit down on the front stoop and keep Rachel and Joey from coming up here when they come back from selling papers." After Zada had told Mr. Lucas what his wife said she sat on the stoop and watched for her brother and sister. This was one time that she was glad they were late coming home. She was sure they would ask questions that she wouldn't be able to answer.

Mrs. Lucas was trying to take Sairy's mind off the pains that were coming closer together. She said, "Sairy, most of my renters call me when the water spigot gets a drip and they can't turn it off, but you waited until all the pipes broke loose." Sairy tried to smile and said, "Rachel and Joey" and stopped as another pain grabbed her. "Don't worry about them. Zada is watching for them and will keep them down stairs until I call her."

The hours dragged by and when Mrs. Lucas thought that Sairy couldn't stand much more a baby girl was born. Shortly after Dr. Adams came and announced that Mrs. Lucas had done a fine job and should give up her job as a landlady and become a midwife.

Zada brought Rachel and Joey in to see their mother and new sister. As they approached the bed, they saw a bundle wrapped in a worn bath towel and a patchwork quilt was pulled up around it casting a shadow across a wrinkled face. Joey and Rachel had not seen a newborn baby, but this one didn't look anything like the six-month old baby that lived across the street. They just stood and stared until Zada said, "Isn't she cute? You can go now, but don't go far."

They left the room and sat at the top of the stairs and looked at each other. Finally Joey whispered something in Rachel's ear and she said, "Yes, I'm sure that's why she looked so funny." They jumped up and bounded down the stairs pounding on every neighbor's door telling them what had happened. Then they ran around the neighborhood shouting, "Our mom has a new nigger baby and she's ugly as sin."

Two neighbors from the second floor that had been in to see the new baby were puzzled by what they saw. As they were going down the stairs, the older lady looked at her friend and said, "Maggie, she's not black or as ugly as I expected." Maggie who was known as the neighborhood gossip was disappointed that she couldn't spread the news about her white neighbor having a black baby. As the woman left, Zada heard them say, "It will probably straighten out but all I saw up there was a bald headed, red and wrinkled kid."

Sairy had decided to name her new daughter in honor of Mrs. Lucas. She would always have a special place in her heart for the woman that helped her when she had no one to turn to. Betsy would be short for Elizabeth. Mrs. Lucas was a little touched and teary when she heard what the baby had been named.

In a couple of weeks Sairy started back to work a few hours in the mornings and she brought ironing home to do in the afternoon. Zada, Rachel and Joey watched Betsy when their mother wasn't home. At first it was fun, but after a while Rachel and Joey missed not being able to run around the neighborhood. Their mom had made it clear that they were not to leave the house while she was working.

Betsy thrived and was soon a favorite of all the renters in the house. Rachel and Joey sold papers in the evening and Zada still worked in the restaurant. She had been promoted from dishwasher to the cook's helper. The evenings were lonely for Sairy and Donnie didn't live close enough to visit very often. She was too busy with the baby and working to make new friends.

When the letter came from Blanche saying that she was coming to visit, the entire family was excited. Rachel had always thought of Aunt Blanche as a person that smiled a lot and made it easy for you to see the funny side of any situation.

Her visit had been a pleasant time for Sairy and the kids, but at the end of two weeks she was getting ready to go home the next morning. Mrs. Lucas came up stairs and told Blanche that the hospital had called and said Sairy had been brought in by the family she was cleaning for that day. She was having pains in her lower back and couldn't straighten up or walk. Blanche told the kids to watch Betsy and she would go to the hospital and see about their mother.

The doctor met Blanche as she entered the hospital and told her that her sister would need an operation.

She couldn't believe what she saw when she entered her sister's ward. There were five other women in the room that she barely noticed, her eyes were focused on her sister. Her face was the color of biscuit dough and when she lifted her hand in hers it felt like it had been dipped in cold spring water. As Sairy saw Blanche she tried to lift her head from the pillow and in a weak voice said, "Sis, see to the kids." Blanche nodded, bit her lip and turned and walked from the room as Sairy closed her eyes and turned her head to the side. A nurse met Blanche in the hall and asked if she was a family member. "Yes, I'm her sister." The nurse said, "Your sister has lost a lot of blood and is very weak, you should call her husband and other close relatives."

When Blanche went back to the house, she told the kids not to worry that their mother was in the hospital where the doctor and nurses would take good care of her until she felt like coming home.

She then went downstairs and knocked on Mrs. Lucas's door. She needed someone to talk with and Mrs. Lucas had a sympathetic ear. After they had talked for two hours, they had a plan of how to handle the situation for the time being. They called up the stairs and asked Zada to come down. They asked her if she thought the Millers would let her stay with them at the restaurant until her mom was home from the hospital. She said it would probably be all right because they had a big house and she would be there to work anytime they needed her. Mrs. Lucas would keep Betsy until she could find her father to come and get her and Blanche would take Rachel and Joey home with her. Blanche knew her father wouldn't be happy to see "Charlie Bonnet's kids" as he referred to them, but she didn't know what else to do.

After Mr. and Mrs. Lucas had had Betsy for a week they finally found where her father was living. They had asked many people before they finally found someone that knew Thelma. John went to see Charlie and he couldn't believe what he said when he told him they were caring for Betsy and where the other kids were. He said, "Zada is old enough to take care of herself. Those two brats ran away when I tried to give them a home and that other kid doesn't even belong to me. Let Sairy figure how to get out of the mess she got herself into."

Sairy was getting better after her operation, but she wouldn't be able to work for a long time. The Lucas's decided that someone had to do something because they couldn't keep the baby indefinitely. "We're not as young as we used to be and I don't have the energy that I did when our kids were little. When the grandchildren come they stay for a little while and then their mother takes them home. This is different." John agreed with his wife and promised that in the morning he would think of something.

He went to the court house the next day and told his story to a lady in the Judge's office. She said she would give the judge the message as soon as he came from the courtroom and she would call him when she had some news.

On the third day after John had been to the court-house they got a call from the Judge himself. He had talked with Charlie and there didn't seem to be any immediate solution to getting him to help his family. Charlie told him, "Put me in jail and I'll stay there until I rot and the wind blows the foul air out the key hole, but I'll still not give them anything. I feel poorly most of the time and I have to save what I have for Thelma and me to get along on. She is the only one that will take care of me." The judge told Mrs. Lucas that they could arrest him for non support, but there still wouldn't be any money coming to Sairy to take care of the children.

Mrs. Lucas called Donnie and asked if she thought the church could help. She told her she would talk to the preacher and ask him to call a meeting of the Deacons. The church decided to adopt the family and help them until Sairy was able to work again.

After a month, Sairy came home from the hospital. She was still weak but determined to get her family back together. Zada came home, and Luke, Donnie's husband, went and brought Rachel and Joey back. Betsy was with her mother most of the time but the women that lived in the building took turns watching her and Sairy was able to rest at times.

Joey and Rachel started selling papers on the street again. They met a lot of people that Sairy would not have approved of, if she had seen them. They did not talk much about what they did away from home. They brought the money from the papers they sold and gave it to their mother. Sairy was grateful because with the money Zada earned at the restaurant and the paper money from Rachel and Joey she bought food.

The church paid the rent and they wore their old clothes. She didn't know what her kids were doing when they were not with her. This worried her but she couldn't get away from the house with Betsy to look after.

She was surprised one day when Joey came into the house wearing a new pair of shoes. "Where on earth did you get those shoes?" Sairy said as she looked at her son. "I bought them. Do you like them?" "Oh they're fine, but where did you get the money?" Sairy said with a troubled look on her face.

"I earned it delivering packages for some men I met at the pool hall," Joey answered in the most grown up voice he could muster. Sairy's heart began to beat faster and she felt weak in the knees as she thought, what is happening to this family? She had heard that some of the men that hung around the pool hall had kids delivering bootleg whiskey for them. The bottles were wrapped in brown paper and most of the kids didn't know what they were carrying.

Joey would be a good person to make deliveries because he knew the layout of the town because of selling papers. She tried not to sound alarmed as she turned to her son and said, "I don't want you to deliver anything else for those men, you are too young to be hanging around a pool room." She didn't tell him what she expected was going on. "Ah Mom, I ain't hurtin' anyone," Joey said as he turned and stomped out of the room.

Those brown slipper shoes with the crepe soles were just the beginning of trouble with her older children. She thought things were going well until one day a strange man knocked on the door. He introduced himself as James Conner, truant officer from the school board. "I'm here to see why Joey and Rachel have not been in school for the past 10 days. I thought they might be sick."

Sairy was at a loss for words, but finally managed to say, "I don't know. I send them every morning and they come home after their paper route is finished." Mr. Conner believed her and he thought to himself as he looked around the meager rooms. "The flat is clean but not much of a place for a woman and four kids to live."

"Mrs. Bonnett, I'll expect your children in school Monday morning and if they aren't and continue to be absent, I'll turn their names over to the proper authorities" Before Sairy could say anything he turned and said, "Good day Mrs. Bonnett," and started down the stairs.

Joey and Rachel came home that evening at the usual time. Their mother asked them, "How was school?" Joey answered, "Same old stuff." Rachel didn't say anything, but continued to play with Betsy like she did when she came in after being out of the house for a while. Sairy didn't know how to handle the problem so she decided to tell them exactly what had happened that afternoon.

She told them the truant officer had come to the house looking for them and what he planned to do if they missed any more school. Rachel and Joey couldn't believe they had been caught skipping school.

Big Al at the pool room had said they were smart kids and didn't need to be tied down in a school room. He told them if they would deliver packages for him and do odd jobs around the pool hall he would teach them to play pool and lots of other fun things that their teachers had probably never heard of.

Rachel and Joey thought it was exciting working for Big Al, except when they had to empty and scrub the spittoons. They promised their mother they would go to school because they didn't like the idea of being turned over to authorities. Neither one knew what would happen to them but they knew it wouldn't be anything good.

Sairy thought everything was straightened out because she hadn't heard anything from the school authorities and they had been coming home on time for the past month. One day when she went down stairs to get the mail, she was surprised to see this important looking letter from the school board. She went back upstairs and sat down at the kitchen table to open it. It was written with a lot of fancy words that Sairy didn't completely understand but she knew that she was supposed to bring Joey for a hearing before a family judge next week.

He had been charged with truancy and stealing a watch from a home while he was delivering bootleg whiskey for Albert Smith. At first Sairy lost control and cried until there were no more tears to come.

She knew she would have to talk to Joey and that she would have to make plans. Since the hearing was in two days, she would keep him home tomorrow and keep an eye on him. The letter hadn't mentioned Rachel, so she was probably going to school. She would ask Zada to stay home on the day of the hearing and watch Betsy. She didn't want any of the neighbors to know where she was going so she couldn't ask them to help her.

Rachel and Joey thought their mom was sick when they came home. Her eyes were red and swollen and the rest of her face was pasty white. Sairy told them to sit down at the table and start talking. "I want to know why I got this letter." She handed them the letter and then waited for one of them to say something. Finally Rachel looked at Joey and said, "I told you that you couldn't trust Big Al." Joey ignored his mother and looked at his sister and said, "But Big Al said that most of the people we made deliveries to would be drunk and not thinking straight and if we saw anything good laying around to pick it up and slip it in our pocket and bring it to him. He promised to pay us extra. I made two whole dollars for bringing that watch in. I didn't think the old guy saw me take the watch. He was staggering around and didn't talk real plain."

Sairy continued to wait and finally Rachel said, "I haven't missed any school, but I don't like it." No one said anything for a while and Joey realized that he had to say something. I went to school for a week, but I couldn't understand the stuff and I hated all of it, so I decided not to go. It was more fun to hang around with the older boys at the pool hall and pick up some money working for Big Al.

The next week was a nightmare for Sairy. Before she knew what was happening Joey was taken away to spend the next part of his life in the State Reform School for boys.

The Judge told Sairy that he would learn a lot and be a better man for the experience. All Sairy could think about was that his father had deserted him and she had failed to keep her son from getting into trouble. She thought about it until her head ached but she couldn't see now she could have done anything differently.

Rachel missed Joey. They had always been close and looked out for each other. Two years had past since

Joey had been sent away and the problems for Sairy and her family continued. She had moved to a cheaper place to live when the church could no longer pay the rent. The church board felt they had an obligation to help more than one family.

She applied for a sewing job at a public-sponsored work program known as the Worker's Project Administration. Most people referred to it as the W.P.A. or the "We Piddle Along Gang." Sairy walked two miles to work each way and made buttonholes by hand in shirts all day. After she caught on to how the supervisor wanted them done, it was a lot easier than scrubbing floors on her hands and knees. The assurance of $40 at the end of each month made life a little easier. Betsy was cared for by Zada, Rachel or whoever was around.

Rachel drifted along like a person lost in a fog after Joey was gone. She lost all interest in school and it wasn't long before Sairy began to get letters from the school authorities. She was seldom home for them to visit so they wrote to her.

Rachel began to run around with older girls and her mother got nothing but a look of defiance when she asked her daughter what she had been doing during the day when she should have been in school.

Sairy was devastated when she received a letter from the juvenile judge asking her to appear in his chambers with Rachel to answer charges that the school authorities had filed against her. It was as if she was again living the nightmare that she had gone through with Joey.

She was given the day off from work with the understanding that she would stay late the rest of the week until she caught up with the work that wouldn't be done while she was away. The sewing center had a quota to meet and the supervisors frowned on anyone being away from the job for any reason.

When Sairy arrived with her daughter at the judge's office, she didn't know what to expect. She couldn't believe her ears when the clerk read the charges: failure to attend school, petty larceny, and loitering around a house of prostitution and incorrigibility. Sairy broke out in a cold sweat and her head felt like it was spinning first one direction and then another.

The judge asked Sairy why she hadn't answered the letters that had been sent and why it took a special delivery notice to get a response from her. Rachel's chin dropped to her chest and Sairy knew immediately that her daughter had destroyed the mail that had been sent to her. She said to the judge, "Ask Rachel."

The next two hours were spent discussing what was best for Rachel and how to accomplish the goal. Sairy couldn't believe she had failed again when Rachel was sentenced to spend time at the State Correctional School for Girls. She was not allowed to go home but was taken by a police woman into another room. The judge explained it was better that way because Rachel might run away and be harmed by some of the company that she had been keeping.

Rachel was "street smart," but she wasn't prepared for what she faced at the correctional school. A bell rang when it was time to get up, to go to the dining room, report for work details and when to be in bed with the lights out. At first she had a buzzing sound going around in her head waiting for the next bell to ring, but after a while she adjusted to the routine. She had a fear of being late for something and being sent to the head matron.

Girls were brought in frequently, while others were sent back home. The school had an agreement with the community leaders that allowed some of the girls to be sent to private home to work a few hours during the day. Mostly they did house cleaning or yard work. Every girl looked forward to the change of being sent out to a job. Anything would be better than being confined to the school all the time. It didn't matter that they never saw the money they earned. Their wages were paid to the school and put into the general operating fund.

Rachel acquired skills that would last a life time. Sewing and other types of needle work were emphasized and her work was soon thought of as the best in her class. She didn't realize it at the time but she was developing personality traits that would stay with her the rest of her life.

She learned to be quiet and not say what she was thinking. The wrong answer could land her in the matron's office with different types of punishment to follow. She seldom smiled and was unable to say much to her mother on the few times she was able to come on visiting days. The school was 50 miles from her home and she knew it was difficult for her mother to come often. Rachel could see the hurt in her mother's eyes and was sorry for the hardships she had caused her, but she couldn't find the words to tell her.

Rachel had been at the school for two years and was considered a quiet girl that fit into the program without problems. When Rachel saw the list on the hall bulletin board of the people that the matron wanted to see the next day, she was puzzled. She couldn't think of what she had done wrong, but knew there was nothing to do but wait.

She was excused from sewing class when it was her turn to go to the office. Mrs. Hardy was a woman of few words and came straight to the point. "Rachel, we have a job for you. Be ready to go tomorrow after breakfast. You will be helping a widow lady with her yard and vegetable garden. Reverend Hawkins will take you and the other girls in the school car and will pick you up and have you back in time for afternoon classes. Do your work well and don't do anything that would disgrace the school. You may go now." Rachel nodded and said, "Yes mam." and left the room.

The next day was the beginning of many jobs for Rachel. The school continued to receive good reports about her work after the lady she had worked for the first day had said, "I never saw anyone that could weed beets and hoe potatoes like that girl." Rachel was sent out about three times a week and she did everything from scrubbing floors to ironing shirts.

Rachel's eighteenth birthday was spent at the school without anyone even saying "Happy Birthday". Presents were never a part of her life so she didn't miss them. The best part of being 18 was that she would be free to leave the school in three years when she was 21.

As Rachel looked out the dormitory window, she saw Mr. Abner coming up the front walk. She had begun cleaning his house every two weeks since his wife passed away last year. He was a quiet man and usually went to do grocery shopping after he told Rachel what he wanted done that day. He had never complained to her and she wondered what she had done wrong that he would come to see Mrs. Hardy. Usually when someone came to complain about a girl it was because she hadn't done the work properly, or worse than anything, she was accused of stealing. Rachel knew that she was the only one that the school had sent to his home, so it must be about her.

An hour later after she had seen Mr. Abner leave, Mrs. Hardy sent for her. Rachel entered the office not knowing what to expect. She stood erect and looked straight ahead as they all had been taught, but she was unable to conceal the fear she felt. "Sit down, Rachel. I have something important to discuss with you." Rachel sat on the edge of the straight back chair and held her sweaty hands in her lap. In all the time she had been at the school she had never sat down in Mrs. Hardy's office.

Every girl knew you were expected to stand erect until dismissed. Her mind wandered from one thing to another. "Maybe I'm being sent to the state prison for women to serve my last three years." She knew that happened sometimes when a girl had done something really bad when they were away from the home working. Jamie, one of Rachel's dormitory mates had recently been transferred for stealing a car and running away.

As usual, Mrs. Hardy came straight to the point. "Rachel Mr. Abner has asked if you would like to become his wife and come live with him. He is lonely since his wife died and he is fond of you. He is 45 years old and is an artist. He will be moving in the near future and would like to take you with him. If you decide to accept his proposal you are free to do so and the final three years of your sentence will be cancelled. While you are in our custody, you do not need the consent of your parents to marry. This is Thursday; report back to me at 9:00 a.m. Monday with your decision. If you decide this is what you want to do, Mr. Abner will be interviewed by the Board of Directors. Give this serious consideration. That's all. You may go now."

Rachel had trouble thinking of anything but the speech Mrs. Hardy had delivered in five minutes that might affect the rest of her life. She knew that some girls had been allowed to marry if they were pregnant when they came to the home and didn't want to give the baby up for adoption, but she hadn't heard of a situation like this.

Mr. Abner was kind and handsome for a man his age. Life with him might not be too bad. Rachel had thought of how she would support herself when she got out in three years. Mrs. Hardy said he was moving. This might be a chance to travel. Rachel had been warned not to discuss this with the other girls. Mrs. Hardy said she didn't want the routine of the school upset by this situation.

On Monday morning when Rachel told Mrs. Hardy that she wanted to be married, it was entirely her decision. She was told by Mrs. Hardy that she would talk with her again after the Board of Directors meet with Mr. Abner. The board approved the marriage if Rachel was still agreeable in thirty days. They suggested that he spend that time getting better acquainted with Rachel.

Rachel remembers that month of her life as a whirl-wind of events. They saw movies, had picnics and listened to classical music on the Victrola. They were married in a quiet ceremony by Reverend Hawkins in the school chapel.

Bill and Rachel were happy. He had a young wife that was a good housekeeper, and she had a man that was kind to her and that she looked up to as a father figure. Bill's job took him to different parts of the country. He restored old pictures and was commissioned to do portraits for wealthy clients. Rachel saw many new places and things and money didn't seem to be a problem.

Zada had come to spend a few days with her sister and at the end of the visit Bill and Rachel were driving her home when something happened that would change Rachel's life forever. They were approaching a railroad crossing and a thick blanket of fog hung in the air. Bill looked up and down the tracts and as he started to drive across a freight train seemed to appear from nowhere with the whistle blowing. Rachel heard the piercing sound and then blacked out. Three days later she blinked as the sun came through a window. When she opened her eyes, she saw Bill and her mother standing near her bed. She was told that she had been sleeping since the wreck.

Bill told her that the car had been dragged along the tracks until the engineer was able to bring the train to a stop. He had escaped with cuts and scratches. Zada had a bad cut on her head and a broken arm and would be in the hospital for a week. He looked away and then said, "Rachel, the doctors think you will need to be in the hospital for a long time so I have made arrangements for an ambulance to transfer you to a hospital near home."

Rachel was to spend the next four months healing from all her injuries. At first Bill came everyday and then he became restless and wanted to move on to another job. They drifted apart and soon after Rachel's discharge from the hospital, Bill asked for a divorce. He said he had met someone that he wanted to spend the rest of his life with.

Rachel was hurt but knew life would go on. She had learned to take care of her self at an early age and the time she had spent at the correctional school had taught her the importance of self discipline.

Her marriage had offered a blanket of security but she wondered what it would have been like to have grown up with people her own age. She tried to imagine how her life would have been if she had stayed with her mother, gone to school and stayed away from the people that had influenced her in so many ways.

In the spring of 1942 the country was at war and Rachel got a job on the assembly line in a defense plant. The hours were long, but she was earning money for the first time since she and Joey had sold papers on the street. She found it hard to meet people and the evenings were lonely.

She usually ate lunch with Virginia, the girl that worked next to her on the line. One day she was telling Rachel about her second job as a hostess in a nightclub. She said one of the girls was going overseas to be with her husband who was in the military and there would be a job opening. Rachel didn't sleep well that night as she tried to make up her mind about getting another job. The next day at lunch she talked with Virginia and decided to go and talk with the manager of the club.

She was hired on the spot and the next two years she worked at two jobs. She was worried when she began to lose weight and was tired most of the time. Virginia was concerned and pleaded with Rachel to go to the doctor for a check up. Two weeks later she walked out of the doctor's office with this advice, "You've worn yourself out and you need a change in your life."

Rachel quit her jobs and started out one morning with her one old brown suitcase. She rode the streetcar to the edge of town and walked to the main highway. She sat down on her suitcase and waited for a ride. This was her first experience at hitch hiking. She had heard people talk about traveling around the country in this manner. She didn't have a destination in mind but just wanted to be on the move and see something different.

She had gotten a couple short rides and had been waiting along the road for a while when a panel truck with the words **JERRY'S FIX IT SHOP**, printed on the side, stopped. Rachel thought, "Maybe I could fix my life if my name was Jerry." She thanked the man as he let her out at his turn off.

She looked up the road and saw lights blinking THE BIG RIG TRUCK STOP and MOTEL. She was hungry and went in and sat at the counter and ordered a hamburger and black coffee. After she finished, she went to the motel office to get a room. When she signed the register, she wrote Jerry Abner from Wadesville. She hadn't lived in Wadesville for many years, but she didn't live anyplace so that town was as good as any. From now on, her name would be Jerry. When she awakened the next morning after a restless night she was tired but to her surprise she was ready for breakfast. She noticed the sign in the window, WAITRESS WANTED as she entered the coffee shop.

While she sat at the counter eating the pancakes and sausage that the waitress had brought, she was thinking, "Do I want to know more about this job?" She had never been a waitress unless you counted the times she took her turn waiting tables at the correctional school. When Dixie was making rounds filling coffee cups, Rachel asked if they still needed a waitress. Dixie said, "We sure do. I'm getting tired of these double shifts since Sue Ann walked out last week. Harry, the boss, will be back in a little while. He went into town to pick up supplies. Can you wait and talk with him?" Rachel nodded her head and said, "Sure."

When Harry pulled into the driveway, Dixie ran from behind the counter and met him at the door. "Need some help?" Harry was a tall gangly man with a receding hair line and a salt and pepper mustache. "Thanks Dixie," Harry said in a quiet voice, "You can bring the carton of napkins. I'll get the rest of it."

Rachel was seated at the counter and waited while Dixie and Harry brought in the rest of the supplies. They both went into the kitchen and Rachel could hear bits of their conversation and knew they were talking about her. Dixie came out first, followed by Harry. She said, "Harry meet

Jerry Abner." "Hi Jerry. Dixie tells me you're looking for work. Ever worked in a restaurant?" "No, but I catch on fast." Harry looked at Jerry and wondered why a good-looking woman like her wasn't married and home taking care of kids. "Where are you from?" Jerry said "All over, I've seen a lot of country." Harry thought to himself, "If I don't get someone, Dixie might walk out, then what would I do?" "Tell you what Jerry, we'll try it for a week and see how it works out.

You can bunk with Dixie in the rooms upstairs for now. Harry had fixed up a two-room apartment over the restaurant for the waitresses to use when they worked long shifts and didn't want to go home or sometimes they lived there all the time as Dixie was now.

The help usually didn't stay very long because the pay was low and the work was hard. Many of the waitresses just worked while they were looking for something better. Rachel didn't have a plan except to face one day at a time. She thought to herself, if I don't like it, I'll just move on.

Dixie was pleasant and Rachel didn't have any problems sharing the rooms with her. For the first couple of days Rachel worked with Dixie and then she was put on a shift by herself. They were seldom in the apartment at the same time.

Rachel settled into the routine and learned to handle the guys that tried to flirt with her. Some of them thought it was their duty to give the new girls a hard time or try to impress them with the tales they told about what they had done and seen as they drove their trucks across country.

Rachel knew most of the customers were away from home and just wanted to talk. Sometimes they didn't see their families more than twice a month. They were hauling freight connected with the war effort and their schedules and routes were irregular.

Rachel became friendly with one of the drivers that had a local route and was in the truck stop almost everyday. Ben had been divorced five years and his three children lived with their mother in another state. Rachel and Ben had been seeing each other away from the restaurant and they both knew that their feelings were more than a passing fancy. This type of relationship was something new to Rachel and she was surprised when Ben asked her to marry him.

She thought of her first marriage as an "arrangement", rather than something that happened when a man and woman fell in love and decided for themselves they wanted to marry. She felt differently about Ben than she had about Bill and she had agreed to marry him. Having her sentence reduced played a big roll in her decision about her first marriage. Two months after Ben proposed, Rachel said yes because she wanted to. She was not trying to escape from anything, but was looking forward to a bright future as Ben's wife.

When Rachel quit her job, Harry and Dixie had a going away party for her. When she had stopped at the truck stop last year, she had only planned to stay long enough to get a pay check. Harry hated to see Rachel go. She was honest and dependable and he could count on her to work extra if someone didn't show up for a shift.

Rachel and Ben were married by a Justice of the Peace at the courthouse and went to live in a trailer near Wadesville. Ben took a job as a long distance driver. He would be home less but the pay was more and the benefits were good. Health insurance and a retirement plan were offered.

Ben was enterprising and was always looking for a way to increase his income. He started a grocery store. The responsibility of running the store was Rachel's because Ben wasn't home much. Rachel learned quickly and the understanding of things like invoices, licenses, and taxes seemed to come easy.

Ben had been made fun of when he was a child because he was overweight. He had found out early in life if he gave his tormentors his lunch or some toy like his pocket knife or marbles they would let him join in the games at recess. This trait carried over into his adult life and many of his acquaintances knew he was a soft touch when they were down on their luck. Ole' Ben was always good for a loan. He would give you the shirt off his back. Many people made no attempt to pay him back and he didn't do anything about it. At the time he might not have realized it, but he was still trying to buy friendship.

After the grocery, Ben branched out to operating a junk yard and selling used car parts. Rachel could soon talk with car mechanics that had been in business for years when they inquired about a part. She knew if she had it, and what make of car it could be used on. They were surprised to find a woman in charge of a place that sold car parts and one that spoke with such authority.

Ben liked to think of himself as a successful business man, but Rachel was the one with organizational skills and the day to day know-how to get things done.

One of Ben's friends wanted to buy the grocery store. He sold it for less than it was worth because he wanted to "help Joe get a start in life." Rachel was furious but said little. She had built the business and was doing well except for the dead beats that wouldn't pay after Ben had extended them credit.

Ben continued to drive truck, but he wanted more. He had dreams of being a landlord so he bought a 12-space trailer park for Rachel to operate. He moved the junk yard and car part business to one end of the land out of view of the renters. Rachel learned to deal with renters' complaints about everything from leaky faucets to neighbors having loud parties. Ben was content to work at driving a truck. The trailer park and the car part business flourished under Rachel's wise management.

When Rachel thought the bank account looked good, someone would come along that was "down on their luck" that Ben just had to help.

Zada had married and had a son. Her husband had disappeared when he knew she was pregnant. With the help of Sairy, Zada had the baby and took care of him. When he was almost three years old, Zada came to Ben and Rachel and asked them if they would take her son to raise. She had been told the day before that she had cancer and only had a short time to live.

Rachel was heart broken. Zada had always been her big sister that she looked up to. Ben and Rachel took Eddie the following week and six months later they adopted him. Lawyers made an attempt to find his father without success. Zada died peacefully on her son's third birthday knowing he would be well cared for.

Rachel had not seen her father for many years and when she read about his death in the newspaper she did not feel like a daughter does when she loses a parent. She thought of him as someone she had known as a child who was responsible for her and Joey being left with grandparents who didn't want them. Thoughts of him taking them from the school yard while their mother was working ran through her mind.

She still resented the time she and Joey had had to wait on Thelma like she was a queen when they lived with their father. Rachel had heard that they had later married. She had no plans to go to the funeral until Joey came to see her. He thought they should attend the service and said, "He was the only dad we ever had and I know he didn't do right by us, but I think we should go."

Ben looked at Rachel and said, "You better give this some thought, you might regret it later." Rachel said, "Okay, I'll go." She thought to herself, "It will be like attending a service for a stranger. I didn't really know him." But the main reason she decided to go was she felt like Joey needed her support.

The funeral was held in a remote country church in the community where he had been born. Snow was falling and the temperature had dropped below freezing. The church was filled to capacity with people that had come "to view the body" as was the custom of the area. Other came because this was a chance to visit with neighbors and friends that they hadn't seen for a while. And some just wanted to see how much Charlie had changed over the years.

Rachel had acknowledged Thelma with a nod as she went in and sat quietly listening to the preacher go on about what a good man he had been. When he began to pray, Rachel closed her eyes and was half asleep in seconds. She suddenly jerked her head up and her eyes flew open as she heard Thelma say in a loud voice, "I wish he would hurry up, my feet are like chunks of ice." Some boys on the back row snickered, and Widow Smith took a coughing spell as the preacher prayed louder. Rachel was mortified and thought to herself, "Why didn't I use my better judgment and stay home?"

Rachel and Joey saw each other frequently, until he took a new job and moved his wife and four children hundreds of miles away. She was glad for him because he was getting a chance to manage a garage that sold and repaired used cars. He had been interested in cars since he and Rachel had their first ride in their Uncle Dave's old truck.

Rachel was known by Ben's friends as the best cook around. He brought truck drivers home with him for a meal without telling Rachel they were coming. She always managed to fix a good meal on short notice, but the drivers would urge Ben to call his wife and tell her they were coming. They hoped she would fix spaghetti with mushrooms in the sauce. This was their favorite dish of all the things she cooked. Rachel enjoyed keeping house and watching Eddie grow.

The years passed and before Rachel could realize it, Ed was married to Mary, a neighborhood girl he had grown up with.

Rachel and Ben had moved from Wadesville when he was given a job as a truck terminal manager in a southern state. Ben was home more often and was making a good salary. He had been with the job five years when he became restless and realized he missed being on the road with the other drivers. The company wanted to keep a good employee, so when the first opening was available he was given a route that ran from the terminal north. Ben was home about every two weeks for a couple of days. Rachel decided she wanted to move back to Wadesville. It was on Ben's route and she would see him as often as she did now. She knew more people there and although Zada was gone, and Ed had moved, Sairy was still there and it would feel more like being home.

Ben agreed, and they bought the trailer park that they had owned before they moved south. The man they bought the park from had not managed it as well as Rachel had, and things were in a run down condition. Rachel began to put things in order and in a short while it was known as the best trailer park for miles around. There was a waiting list of people who wanted to rent either a furnished trailer or a space to set their own trailer.

Sairy had been in failing health and had gone to live with Betsy and her family before Rachel had moved back to Wadesville. Sairy was in bed most of the time the last two years of her life, and someone had to be with her at all times. Rachel would hire someone to work at the trailer park for a few days and she would go help Betsy care for their mother.

It tore at Rachel's heart to see this woman slowly waste away and to know that she would never be better. She thought of the struggle her mother had had to provide food, a place to live, and her constant efforts to keep them all together.

On the morning Betsy had called and said their mother had died peacefully in her sleep, Rachel was both relieved and sad. Relieved because her mother was now free of pain, and sad because of the empty feeling that gripped her whole body.

Rachel had long ago made peace with her mother about the trouble she had caused her when she was a young girl. Sairy had told her, "I love you and know that the future will be better for you."

As she sat in the chapel of the funeral home and listened to the minister offer words of comfort to the family, she had a completely different feeling than she had when she went with Joey to their father's funeral.

Rachel was devoted to her four granddaughters and when Mary was hospitalized after a car wreck, they stayed with her and Ben for a while. Mary Lou, named for her mother, seemed to be the most outgoing of the group. She was next to the youngest but the others seemed to look up to her as their leader.

Ben's health was failing. He had many problems related to his weight. He tried not to think about his health and when someone asked how he felt, he would answer, "I'm fine." Then he would change the subject.

He had to face reality when he failed his yearly health checkup which was necessary for all interstate truck drivers. He retired early and got a monthly check from the trucking company. He was home now and took an active part in the trailer park business.

Rachel stood quietly by and watched them go deeper in debt as Ben continued to help anyone that asked. He wasn't concerned when someone was late with their rent or damaged something in one of the trailers and refused to pay for it. He always made excuses for them and Rachel thought to herself, "He wants to be looked up to and is still trying to buy friendship."

Because Rachel had established a good relationship with the bank, they were able to get a loan to get them out of the financial mess Ben had created.

In spite of the problems with money that seemed to be with them constantly, Ben held a special place in Rachel's heart. Most of her life she had kept quiet to avoid trouble and her relationship with Ben was no different.

Five years after Ben retired, he died of a massive heart attack, that the doctor said was a result of him weighing three times what he should have weighed.

Rachel tried for a year to straighten out her financial affairs. It seemed like an impossible task. Bills kept popping up that Ben hadn't told her about and he failed to sign the proper papers for her to get any of his retirement benefits after his death. She finally decided to sell the trailer park at a loss and take what money was left after paying bills and move close to Joey and his family.

Rachel remembers the next five years of her life as a pleasant time. Joey and his family were her security. She had her own apartment and met many new friends at the Senior Citizen Center. Joey's daughters looked on her as a combination aunt and grandmother.

Her only worry was Joey's health. He had had heart surgery and his physical activity was limited. He was still able to work at his job because the company had assigned him to writing contracts and greeting people when they came in to look at cars to buy.

Rachel had been with Joey and his family on a week's vacation. They had camped in the mountains and everyone had come home with a feeling of being at peace with the world.

Rachel's world collapsed when she picked up the phone three days later and heard her niece Patty scream, "Aunt Rachel, Daddy is dead. Mom found him in his chair in the living room this morning. She thought he was just having a restless night and had gotten up to watch television. She told me to call an ambulance and then she fainted. Carolyn ran next door to get Mrs. Gonzales." Rachel interrupted her niece and said, "I'll be there in five minutes." She hung up the phone and left.

When she arrived, two men from the emergency squad were loading a cot into the ambulance. She ran into the house and found Abbie sitting on the couch with Patty and Carolyn sitting at her feet with their heads resting in her lap.

Mrs. Gonzales had fixed hot chocolate and was urging Abbie to have some.

Rachel was busy the next few weeks helping Abbie and dealing with her own grief. It was hard for her to describe how she felt about Joey. He had been a part of her life for as long as she could remember. Events of the past kept popping up in her mind, but the one she remembered most vividly was when she and Joey had hidden under the lilac bush waiting for each other to shrink after they had eaten peppermint sticks that they had stolen from their dad's store.

With Joey gone, Rachel was restless and homesick for Ed and her grandchildren and she decided to move back to Wadesville.

Ed found her a trailer to rent and she managed to get by on her monthly social security check. When she developed health problems and needed to take medicine there wasn't always money to buy what the doctor prescribed. Rachel handled the problem by cutting back on expensive food items like meat. She bought her clothing at rummage sales and stood in line every month when the Salvation Army passed out food to the needy.

She tried not to think of what her life might have been if Ben had not given their money away trying to buy friendship. She was bitter about the life style she was forced to lead. Ben was gone so she struck out at the people around her.

She criticized everyone and refused to see the good points of the people that tried to be her friends. She built a shell around herself and often said that FeFe, her dog was the only one that cared for her. She was the domineering one and had found something that had to take orders from her.

She had been back in Wadesville for 13 years and recently Ed and Betsy checked on her frequently. She refused to live in a nursing home or to have anyone live in the house with her.

Since the day Mr. Bosley had called Ed when Rachel had been looking for her mother and Austin, he had visited her often. Sometimes he would find her in the floor where she had fallen. The doctor said that the dizzy spells that caused her to fall were brought on by hardening of the arteries that lead to the brain and nothing much could be done about it.

The day that Ed sent her to the hospital in an ambulance she had been lying on a floor furnace vent for several hours. When she was ready to be discharged, the doctor said she could not live alone again. She couldn't remember things and often had hallucinations of other people being in the house with her. Betsy who had been appointed to look after Rachel's affairs was making arrangements for her to live in a nursing home, when Mary Lou, Ed's daughter decided to take her into her home and care for her.

Rachel's is now surrounded by a loving family, her mind continues to be mixed up and she lives in a world of make-believe where children are given yellow bananas and red peppermint sticks every day and no one has to swallow snuff to keep a soul from burning in hell.